Dedication

For Dan, Brian, Ellen and Annie.

Other Books by Judi Curtin

The Lissadell series

Lily at Lissadell

The 'Molly & Beth' series

Time After Time

Stand By Me

You've Got A Friend

The 'Alice & Megan' series

Alice Next Door

Alice Again

Don't Ask Alice

Alice in the Middle

Bonjour Alice

Alice & Megan Forever

Alice to the Rescue

Viva Alice!

Alice & Megan's Cookbook

The 'Eva' Series

Eva's Journey

Eva's Holiday

Leave it to Eva

Eva and the Hidden Diary

Only Eva

Judi Curtin

Lily Steps Up

A Lissadell Story

THE O'BRIEN PRESS
DUBLIN

First published 2020 by
The O'Brien Press Ltd,
12 Terenure Road East, Rathgar,
Dublin 6, D06 HD27 Ireland.

Tel: +353 1 4923333; Fax: +353 1 4922777

E-mail: books@obrien.ie
Website: www.obrien.ie

The O'Brien Press is a member of Publishing Ireland
ISBN: 978-1-78849-209-6
Text © copyright Judi Curtin 2020
Copyright for typesetting, layout, editing, design
© The O'Brien Press Ltd

1 3 5 7 8 6 4 2
20 22 23 21

Internal illustration, cover design and cover illustration by Rachel Corcoran.
Internal design by Emma Byrne.
Printed and bound by Norhaven Paperback A/S, Denmark.
The paper in this book is produced using pulp from managed forests.

Published in

DUBLIN
UNESCO
City of Literature

Chapter One

'And they all lived happily ever after.'

She closed the storybook and sat back on her bed with a big sigh.

'Well done, Nellie!' I said giving her a hug. 'That was wonderful. You read a whole book all by yourself.'

The book was made for little children, and it had taken Nellie many days to get to the end, stumbling over the bigger, unfamiliar words. That didn't matter though. Nellie didn't have much schooling, so she was very proud of herself now.

'I could never have done this without you,' she said. 'Oh, Lily, whatever would I have done if you hadn't

come to work here with me? You've changed my life.'

I was embarrassed. It was true, I *had* taught her to read – but that was easy to do, as she was so clever and eager to learn. I wished I could do more to change her life though.

Sometimes I felt like crying when I thought of all the bad things that had happened to Nellie. After her mam and dad died when she was little, Nellie and her two sisters were sent to the workhouse. When they got there, Nellie was separated from her sisters, and she never saw them again. Now the poor girl had no idea where they were, or even if they were still alive. That meant she had no family at all to care for her or love her – but how could I fix that? I couldn't bring her mam and dad back, and how could a poor housemaid like me even begin to search for her sisters? Teaching Nellie to read was the best I could do, but it didn't seem like enough.

Nellie climbed under her blankets and put the book on her locker.

'I'm going to start reading it again tomorrow,' she said. 'And I'm going to read it every day until I can do all the pages without a single mistake.'

'Good idea,' I said, as I put out the gas-light and climbed into my own bed. 'And then I can get more books from the nursery and help you with those. Before long you'll be reading the newspaper and all the big, hard books in the library.'

'Thank you, Lily,' she said sleepily and a few minutes later I could tell from her breathing that she was fast asleep.

I couldn't sleep, as I thought back to my first days at Lissadell House many months ago. Back then, Nellie was grumpy, and mean to me. Now I knew her better and understood why she had been like that. Nowadays she was very sweet to me and rarely complained about anything. Nowadays she was a very dear friend.

Lissadell was Nellie's whole life, but I knew that, deep down, she wanted what I had. She wanted a family of her own.

As I lay there in the darkness, I made up my mind that I was going to help my friend – only I had no idea how I was going to do it.

* * *

My back hurt and my knees were starting to go numb. Outside it was a beautiful sunny day, and I wanted to cry as I thought how much I'd love to be running in the fields near home, with my brothers and my darling little sisters. I thought how much I'd love to throw myself into Mam's arms, and have her laugh as she smoothed my windblown hair. I couldn't do those things though. I was alone in this cold, narrow place.

It was my turn to scrub the servants' staircase – a job Nellie and I both hated. This staircase was dark and twisty and nothing like the fancy one the family used. The edges of the steps had grooves on them and there they needed extra scrubbing. (Mrs Bailey, the housekeeper, would certainly check, and I'd be

in trouble if I missed even a tiny speck of dirt.) The middle part of each step was smooth, though – worn away by the feet of generations of servants like me.

As I scrubbed, I thought about my days at school, and how happy I had been then. I used to watch the Master, and Miss O'Brien, and imagine that one day I'd be a teacher just like them. How I wanted to help all the little children to read and write and sing and sew!

I still had that dream, but every day it seemed further away. How would Mam or I ever save up enough money so I could go away to teaching college?

* * *

I was only half finished my job when I heard the skip of feet coming down the stairs towards me.

'*There* you are, Lily,' said Maeve. 'I've been looking everywhere for you.'

I smiled – that was the trouble with living in a

huge house like Lissadell, it was easy to get lost.

'Hello, Maeve,' I said.

As I stood up, rubbing my back, I began to feel ashamed. My apron was wrinkled and dusty, and as usual I could feel strands of my hair falling from my white cap. Maeve's long, wavy hair was shiny and newly brushed, and she was wearing a perfect dress of pink satin and lace. It was hard to forget that Maeve was a member of the family who owned Lissadell House, while I was only a servant. Then I gave myself a little shake, as I remembered what my lovely daddy used to say – 'We might be poor, Lily, but you're as good as everyone else on this green earth, never forget that.' So I smoothed my apron and stood up taller and smiled at my friend.

'I didn't know you were here,' I said. 'I thought you were at your grandmother's house.'

'I was there until lunchtime,' she said. 'I had lessons this morning, and it was terrible. My friend Stella is sick, so Miss Clayton had me all to herself. She was

in a foul temper and made me do the most horrible mathematics over and over again until my head hurt. I wanted to throw the textbook at her.'

I laughed at the thought. 'But you didn't do it?'

'No. Mother has threatened that if I misbehave again, she will have me sent away to boarding school, and if she does that, I will scream and kick and cry and ...'

I stopped listening for a second. I didn't know much about boarding school, but I'd have loved to go to any kind of school at all. There were so many books I wanted to read and so many things I wanted to learn.

'... and I'll run away, and if Mother sends me back, I'll run away again. I *won't* go to boarding school, I simply won't.'

'I'm sure she wouldn't force you to go, Maeve,' I said, trying to soothe her. I didn't believe my own words though. Maeve's mother, Countess Markievicz, was a brave woman – and a bit terrifying too. I couldn't

imagine *anyone* stopping her from doing something once she had made up her mind.

'How is your mother?' I asked trying to change the subject.

'Busy as usual,' said Maeve. She spoke as if she didn't care, but that was only an act. Everyone at Lissadell loved Maeve, and spoiled her, but I knew she missed her mam who lived in Dublin.

'Uncle Joss and Aunt Mary won't talk about Mother of course,' she continued. 'But I've been reading about her in the newspaper. She's working very hard with Na Fianna Eireann.'

'What's that?'

'It's an organisation for boys – a little like the Boy Scouts.'

That didn't help me as I didn't know what Boy Scouts were either. 'What do they do?'

'They have meetings, and do things like marching up and down and pretending to have guns – it sounds very boring to me.'

'Me too.'

'Mother is one of the leaders, and she's working on a handbook for them. In her last letter she told me she's done some of the drawings.' She started to laugh. 'Uncle Joss is always saying Mother should have ladylike hobbies like drawing – but I don't think that is quite what he had in mind.'

'Your mother has such an interesting life,' I said.

'*Too* interesting, if you ask me,' said Maeve. 'Anyway, I've told Mrs Bailey I need you to help me with my painting, so you can leave that cleaning and come with me.'

'But ...' I pointed at the half-scrubbed staircase.

'Don't worry about that. Maybe Nellie will have time to do it.'

'That's not fair.'

'Why? She never seems to mind when you miss work to spend time with me.'

That was true. Even though Nellie got very cross when she thought anyone else wasn't doing their fair

share of work, she never complained about Maeve and me.

'She's my dear friend,' I said. 'And that's why I can't take advantage of her. I'll go to Mrs Bailey now, and tell her I'll finish the stairs later. I'll see you in your bedroom in a few minutes?'

'No. It's too nice to be inside. I'm going to paint outside today. I'll see you in the *porte cochere* in ten minutes.'

So I ran back downstairs with my mop and bucket and scrubbing brush, feeling as if I had been set free from prison.

Chapter Two

I'd never heard of a *porte cochere* before I got to Lissadell, but now I was used to the place with the huge doors, where the motorcar would let out passengers and they'd be protected from the wind and rain. I stood there and tried to be invisible as I waited for my friend. Daddy was right when he said I was as good as everyone else, but there were lots of rules in Lissadell House and, as usual, Maeve was asking me to break most of them. I wasn't supposed to speak to any of the family unless they spoke to me first. I wasn't supposed to give up jobs when they were only half-done, and run off into the garden with Maeve. I was expected to use the servants' entrance, and was only allowed to be in the *porte cochere* if it needed sweeping or mopping.

Albert, the driver, was whistling as he polished the

already shiny motor car. A second later, the front door opened and Sir Josslyn and Lady Mary came down the steps. Sir Josslyn nodded at me and climbed into the front seat of the car. Lady Mary stopped and gave me a warm smile. She looked like a princess in her fancy coat, and a hat with green feathers. She smelled of soap and violets.

'Hello, Lily, she said, in her beautiful soft voice. 'How are you today?'

'I'm very well, Lady Mary,' I said. 'Thank you for asking.'

I tried to keep my voice from shaking. What if she asked why I was standing in the *porte cochere*, and not a bucket or a mop in sight?

But she was still smiling, and she didn't seem to be in a hurry. 'And how is your sewing coming along? Did you finish the dresses for your little sisters?'

'Almost, Lady Mary,' I said. 'I only have to put the buttons on Anne's and then they will be ready. The girls will love them.'

'I am sure they will. You are the most gifted needleworker I have seen for quite a long time.'

I felt dizzy, from being praised by such a fine lady. 'Oh, thank you, Lady Mary,' I said. 'Thank you for saying that and thank you for giving me the fabric and the buttons and the thread and the lace and ...'

She smiled and I understood she had heard enough. 'You are very welcome,' she said. 'I hope you haven't forgotten about the home industries show. You should make some things and have them ready to exhibit. I am sure you will do marvellously well.'

Of course I hadn't forgotten the home industries show! The first prize was three shillings, and even the third prize of a shilling would have been wonderful to me.

'Thank you, Lady Mary,' I said.

'Please help yourself from the fabric store cupboard – now that I think of it, there is some very nice velvet there, left over from my winter suits. You could take some of that, and make some more dresses for your

sisters – and enter one in the home industries show.'

'Velvet!' I whispered.

Before I came to Lissadell, I had never even touched a piece of velvet, and the thought of my little sisters actually owning velvet dresses …! For a second I wondered where they would even keep them – Mam's little cottage didn't have wardrobes and dressing rooms like the ones at Lissadell.

'They would love that so much,' I said. 'They would be the sweetest girls in the whole village – and I promise they would keep them for Sunday best and …'

I put my hand over my mouth to stop myself from chattering on, as Lady Mary smiled at me and climbed into the back of the car. Albert closed the door behind her. He winked at me as he sat into his own seat, and with a roar of the engine, they drove away.

Just then the door opened again and Maeve appeared, staggering under the weight of a huge tartan rug, an easel, a box of paints and a picnic

18

basket. I smiled. Who cared about rules? Life was always more fun when Maeve was around.

* * *

Ten minutes later, the two of us were settled under a huge horse chestnut tree. I took off my frilly white cap and let the warm breeze toss my hair. I pulled my boots off and wriggled my toes in the sunshine. I tried not to wonder when I'd find time to darn the hole on the big toe of one of my stockings. Then I lay back on the soft rug and gazed up at the branches high over my head. It was springtime and the young leaves were fresh and green and new. I closed my eyes and tried to imagine a world where I'd never again have to scrub a stairs or clean out a dirty fireplace. I tried to imagine a world where I could lie on a rug for as long as I liked, any time I wanted.

Why couldn't I have a rich uncle in America who'd die and leave me hundreds of pounds?

How wonderful it would be if I could get a house for me and Mam and the little ones – with two bedrooms so Mam wouldn't have to sleep in the kitchen any more?

How wonderful if I could afford to train to be a teacher?

I lay there for a long time, enjoying the moment, dreaming impossible dreams.

* * *

Maeve tickled my nose with a piece of grass and I sat up quickly.

The easel and the paint-box were thrown carelessly on the grass beside us.

'When are you going to start painting, Maeve?' I said. 'Should I fix my hair? Put my boots and cap back on? Would you like me to sit or stand up?'

Maeve laughed, as I knew she would. 'I don't feel like painting today,' she said.

Maeve never felt like painting – it was only an excuse so the two of us could spend some time together – an excuse I was very happy to go along with.

'Tell me about Winnie and Anne,' she said.

I smiled. Maeve had lots of sweet little cousins, but she always seemed more interested in my brothers and sisters who she'd never even met.

'Winnie's cough is nearly gone, and when I was home last week, her cheeks were rosy. The medicine I can afford to buy now helps her, but I think mostly she's better because of all the food that Cook lets me bring home. Mam's so grateful for how kind your family has been to us.'

Maeve's cheeks went pink. I'd forgotten how embarrassed she got when I said things like that. 'And how is Anne?' she asked.

'Anne is as bold as ever,' I said. 'But she's as bright as a button. She knows all her letters now, and most of her numbers too.'

Talking about my family made me feel strange – sad and happy at the same time. I knew I was lucky to have a good job in Lissadell, but I couldn't get used to seeing my family just once a week. How could I complain to Maeve, though? She hardly ever saw her mam, and her daddy was far away in Europe.

We chatted for a long time, sharing stories from our different worlds. Then my tummy rumbled, and I gazed longingly at the picnic basket. Cook loved Maeve, and always gave her delicious treats.

Maeve opened the basket and lay a heap of treasures on the good linen napkins. There were sandwiches with no crusts, and little ginger biscuits, and chocolate sweets, and scones with jam and cream and bottles of fresh lemonade. I ate until I was ready to burst, and for a while I could imagine that I was a fine lady with nothing to do except enjoy myself.

Then I noticed that the air had begun to chill and the sun was sinking low in the sky.

'I'm going to be in so much trouble, I said, jump-

ing up and throwing the scraps into the basket. 'Mrs Bailey will kill me for staying out so long. I have to finish the stairs and light the bedroom fires and polish the glasses and set the table for dinner and—'

'I'm sorry,' said Maeve. 'I'll tell her it's all my fault.'

I knew she'd do exactly that, but I also knew that Mrs Bailey would smile at Maeve and say it didn't matter, but later she'd be extra snappy with me.

We folded the rug, picked up the basket and the unused easel and paints, and hurried towards the house.

'When will I see you again?' I asked. Maeve still had her own room at Lissadell, but mostly she stayed with her grandmother, Gaga, who lived at Ardeevin, a few miles away.

'Oh, not for ages and ages. We're all going away to stay with my Aunt Mabel in England. We'll be gone for three weeks. Didn't I tell you?'

I was so surprised, I stopped walking. If I were going to England, I'd have been shouting it from the

rooftops, and getting it published in the *Sligo Champion*. How could Maeve be so casual about such a big thing?

But then I remembered that she'd been to England lots of times before, and for her it was no more exciting than a trip to the next village.

'No, you didn't tell me,' I said, feeling a bit cross, both because Maeve wasn't excited about the trip, and because I was going to miss her so much. 'Who's going?'

'Everyone – Uncle Joss and Aunt Mary and the children and Gaga and me.'

'But I'll see you again before you go?'

'I don't think so. Gaga says I must have extra lessons to make up for all the time I'll be away, so I'm going back to Ardeevin tonight. Gaga and I will leave from there, and meet everyone else in Dublin, and travel on from there together.'

Now I felt like crying. Dublin sounded so far away and exotic – I could hardly even imagine that it was

a real place.

And then I wasn't cross any more, as I thought of something wonderful. 'If all the family is away, does that mean that Nellie and I and all the other servants have a holiday too? We won't have much work to do – no bedrooms to clean, except our own, no fires to light, no fancy drawing rooms to tidy. Do you know, Maeve, do we have a holiday too?'

'I'm sorry, Lily. When we're on holidays, well, we're on holidays, and I don't know what happens in Lissadell while we're gone. I hope you have a holiday, Lily, I really do, but I don't actually know.'

* * *

I didn't get a chance to talk to Nellie until bedtime. I had worked late, finishing the servants' stairs, so Nellie had put out the light by the time I got to our little room. The light that came in from the passageway was just enough for me to see her curled

up under the blankets. I smiled when I saw one of Master Michael's storybooks still open on the bed beside her. No matter how tired she was, she always read a few lines before settling down for the night.

'Did you have a nice time with Maeve?' she asked sleepily.

I wanted to hug her. While I'd been lying on a rug in the sunshine, eating treats, Nellie had been working hard, with barely a break to catch her breath, but she wasn't jealous or anything. She really seemed to care about me having a nice time.

'I had a lovely afternoon,' I said. 'But tell me, Nellie, did you know that the whole family is going away to England next week?'

'Yes,' she said. 'Isabelle mentioned it yesterday. She's already busy sorting out the babies' clothes, and packing their little bags.'

'But why didn't you tell me?'

'I didn't think you'd care. I'm sorry you'll miss Maeve, but otherwise ...'

'But when they're gone, do we ...?' Suddenly I felt stupid. What had I been thinking? If the servants were getting a holiday, they'd all be happy and excited. If we were getting a holiday I'd know it by now.

'Do we what?' asked Nellie.

'Do we ... I mean, if they're gone what are we supposed to do all day long?'

I'd given up on the idea of a holiday, but maybe a few hours extra in bed every morning was still a possibility?

Now Nellie sat up, and in the dim light I could see her long red curls tumbling around her shoulders.

'Oh, Lily,' she said. 'I'm sorry. This is all new to you. You weren't here the last time they went away, were you? It's not much fun, I can tell you that.'

'But ...'

'When the family goes away, we have to clean the house from top to bottom.'

'We do that every day anyway, don't we?'

'This is different. We have to clean every single

thing in the house. Mrs Bailey will have lists as long as her arm, and she'll follow us around the place like a wild woman, pointing at things we've missed and having conniptions. Oh, Lily, I get tired even thinking about it.'

Nellie gave a big yawn and lay down again. I wasn't sure I understood what she was saying – as far as I could see, the house was clean enough. What did I know though? I was only an under-housemaid, and I had to do what I was told.

Chapter Three

At last the big day arrived and Mr Kilgallon, the butler, told all the servants to line up in the hallway. We watched in silence as the footmen carried the last of the suitcases and trunks out of the house.

'Looks as if they're going away for three years,' whispered Nellie, and I thought I'd choke from trying not to laugh. She was right, though – the things they were taking would barely fit into my whole house. I thought that England must be a strange place if the family had to bring so many supplies to survive a few weeks there.

Lady Mary and Sir Josslyn came down the big stairs, looking wonderful in their warm travelling clothes. Behind them came the nurse, with baby Brian in her arms, and Isabelle, the children's maid who was carrying Bridget. Isabelle was my friend,

and she had been very kind to me when I arrived at Lissadell. I knew I'd miss her when she was away.

Michael and Hugh were trailing behind everyone else. Poor little Hugh was sobbing. He looked tired and confused, as if he'd have been happier staying in the nursery playing with his toy soldiers. I wanted to give him a big hug, but I knew that wasn't the right thing to do, so I smiled at him instead, hoping that would help.

Sir Josslyn gave a little speech, saying how he hoped we would all keep well, and that he knew we would work hard while they were gone. When he finished I started to clap, but no one else joined in. Mr Kilgallon glared at me, so I pretended I'd been trying to catch a fly between my palms, making Nellie giggle.

Lady Mary shook everyone's hand, as if she were saying goodbye to us forever. Then she and Sir Josslyn and the children got into the motor car. There wasn't room for Isabelle and the nurse, so they travelled on the pony and carriage, squashing themselves in amongst

the trunks and suitcases and presents for the family in England. I'd have felt sorry for them, except that they were going to Dublin and England and places I could only dream of. I'd happily have travelled on the back of a smelly old pig-cart for the opportunity they had.

The little procession set off on their journey and the servants stood there for a second, before Mr Kilgallon clapped his hands.

'No holiday for us,' he said. 'Time to set to work. No dilly-dallying now.'

I looked up to see Mrs Bailey walking towards me with a determined look in her eye and a long sheet of paper in her hand.

'Nellie, Lily,' she said. 'Gather your traps. You're starting in Lady Mary's room, so I'll see you there in five minutes.'

* * *

The next few days were the longest of my whole

life. The footmen took down the curtains from each bedroom, and carried them outside and laid them across the clothes lines. There Nellie and I had to beat them until our backs were breaking. When that was done, all the mattresses and bedding were carried outside and wiped and brushed.

While these were airing, Nellie and I had to scrub every inch of every room – under the beds and inside the wardrobes and in dark corners I'd never have thought of cleaning. All the windowpanes had to be polished with vinegar and old newspapers, and I wondered if my fingers were going to be black forevermore. Every ten minutes, Mrs Bailey appeared, criticising and complaining and saying that we weren't working hard enough.

On the third day, Nellie and I emptied Maeve's wardrobe so we could clean it. As we were putting the beautiful clothes back, I pointed out a dress, 'This is the one I wore the first time Maeve said she wanted to paint me.'

'I bet it was lovely on you,' said Nellie as she picked up another dress and held the bright blue fabric to her cheek. 'I think this is the softest thing I have ever touched,' she sighed.

The blue of the dress matched her eyes perfectly, and made her curls shine like polished copper.

'Oh, Nellie!' I didn't know how to continue. It was hard to believe that this sweet, smiling girl had been so mean and grumpy when I first knew her. Now I loved her and wanted her to have everything in the world.

'What?' she asked, as she put the dress back in the wardrobe and picked up our brushes and mops.

'Don't you sometimes think that life is unfair? Maeve has wardrobes full of dresses she hardly ever wears, and you and I ...'

'I know,' she said, as we went out of the room. 'Life *is* unfair, but complaining about it doesn't make it any better. I tell myself every day how lucky I am to be here at Lissadell.'

'Lissadell is a beautiful house, and the Gore-Booths are kind – but don't you think the endless work ...?'

'I don't mind the work too much – I quite like making things shiny and clean.'

I smiled at her. 'I wish I could be like that.'

'I try to be happy with what I have, and who knows, maybe there are great things waiting around the corner for both of us?'

'Knowing our luck, the only thing waiting around the corner for us will be Mrs Bailey,' I said.

I jumped as Mrs Bailey appeared out of Gaga's bedroom. 'You were saying, Lily?' she said.

'Oh, er, I was only saying I hoped you'd be here so we could tell you we're finished in Miss Maeve's bedroom.'

'Hmmm,' said Mrs Bailey. 'Is that a fact?'

I looked at the floor and bit my tongue and didn't answer. Sometimes being an under-housemaid was very hard.

Chapter Four

On Friday night I fell into bed feeling that I would never again be able to move, but on Saturday morning I jumped up like a newborn lamb, ready to enjoy every moment of my day off.

I took my sewing basket from under the bed, and pulled out the dress I was making for my little sister, Anne. I smoothed the soft fabric and smiled. Every stitch was perfect – even the hard, fancy ones on the sleeves. When we were at school, my friend Hanora and I were the very best at sewing, and Miss O'Brien made pets of us. Often Hanora and I stayed back when everyone else went home and she showed us stitches that the other girls would never have been able for. Because of Miss O'Brien, and Mam, who still helped me, I could sew nearly anything.

I threaded my needle and began to sew the first

tiny yellow button in place.

Nellie opened her eyes. 'Why are you sewing now?' she asked. 'You never sew on Saturdays, you're in such a hurry to get home to your family.'

'I know. I'm dying to get on the road, but Winnie's dress has been finished for ages, and I only have to put the buttons on Anne's. It's going to be such a great surprise for them, I can't wait any more.'

'I'm excited for them too,' said Nellie. 'I can picture their happy faces. They sound like such sweet little girls.'

Saturday was the day I lived for, the only day I could spend with my family. Nellie didn't have that, though – her whole world was in Lissadell.

Life was so unfair!

'I'll help you to get ready,' said Nellie, jumping out of bed. 'So you'll get home faster.'

She opened our little shared wardrobe and began to lay out my clothes for me – my Sunday best dress, and my clean stockings and my coat.

'Thank you, Nellie,' I said. 'You're a good friend.'

* * *

It was a bright and breezy day and I sang to myself as I walked along the shore. My basket was heavy, but I didn't care. Cook had given me a big bunch of carrots, a lump of cheese, a loaf of fresh bread and some freshly churned butter. She had added a little bag of ginger biscuits, because I had once told her that my brothers loved them.

The dresses for Winnie and Anne were folded up in tissue paper and balanced on top of everything, and even thinking about them made me smile. Sometimes I hated my work in Lissadell, but without it, I would never have such beautiful presents for my favourite little girls in the world.

* * *

Denis and Jimmy were playing on the road in front of the house. They didn't run to hug me anymore, in case any of their friends were nearby, but their smiles told me they were glad to see me.

'Mam,' shouted Jimmy. 'Lily's here. Lily's here.'

Mam came to the door, wiping her hands on her old familiar worn-out apron. I ran into her safe, warm arms and she held me for a long time. That first hug on a Saturday was the best moment of my whole week, and I wanted it to go on and on. In Lissadell, I had to act like a grown-up, but when I came home, I was still Mam's little girl, and I knew that would never, ever change.

Winnie was pulling at my dress, and Anne was jumping up and down beside her.

'What's in the basket?' said Anne.

'Basket for Winnie?' said Winnie.

I let go of Mam and stooped down to hug the little girls. They clung on, wriggling and fighting to get the best grip on me.

'Were you good for Mam this week?' I asked when they finally let me go. Winnie was a little pet from the first day she was born, but Anne had a wild streak – she tried very hard to be good, but sometimes the effort was too much for her.

'They were as good as gold,' said Mam, smiling at me. She already knew what the surprise was. Months ago, when the girls were napping, she had helped me with the first dress, showing me how to do the hard parts like putting in the sleeves and gathering up the waist.

'Well, then, girls,' I said. 'In that case I have a big surprise for each of you.'

Now Winnie and Anne were jumping up and down with excitement, and Anne was making little squeaky noises, and I wanted the special moment to last forever.

I took the parcel from the basket and slowly unwrapped the tissue paper. I shook out the dresses and handed one to each girl. They held the dresses in

their tiny hands and didn't say a single word. I was so disappointed. What was wrong? These were the best things I had ever made. The fabric Lady Mary gave me was soft and fine and perfect for a little girl. I had sewn and sewn, all through dark and cold winter nights. Why didn't they like them?

In the end, when Anne spoke, her voice was a whisper so quiet I had to lean closer to catch the words.

'For me?'

'For me?' echoed her little sister.

At last I understood. They would have been happy with a ginger biscuit each, and the idea of a new dress was too much for them to take in.

I laughed. 'Yes, of course they are for you, you sillies. Now let's try them on and see how you look.'

The girls were already wriggling out of their old, faded dresses, and seconds later they were parading around in the new ones.

I felt tears coming to my eyes. The dresses fitted perfectly, and the girls looked like two sweet little

angels. I wished they could each have a hundred dresses, in every colour of the rainbow.

Mam hugged me. 'You're the best big sister in the world.'

'That's a coincidence,' I said. 'Because I've got the best mam in the world too.'

* * *

The boys came in as Mam was emptying the basket and exclaiming over all the food that Cook had sent. When they saw the ginger biscuits, they both did a little dance of joy. I laughed. Every time I came home they seemed more grown up, and I was happy to see that they were still little boys at heart.

When the food was put away safely in the pantry, the girls wanted to go outside to play in the front yard. Mam warned them a hundred times about keeping their new dresses clean, and Denis and Jimmy went outside to keep an eye on them as they played.

Mam and I sat by the fire. I loved those quiet moments when it was just the two of us together, chatting about this and that.

'How is your friend?' she asked.

I don't keep many secrets from Mam, but didn't dare to tell her that I was friends with Maeve. In her eyes, I had no business being friends with anyone rich. She thought that kind of thing would lead to trouble for me.

'Who?' I asked, trying not to look guilty.

'Nellie – your friend Nellie who you told me about. How is she these days?'

'Oh, my friend Nellie,' I said, relieved. 'She's well. She's getting very good at reading and she still wears the mittens you made her at Christmas – even when it's not cold at all.'

Mam smiled. 'She sounds like a sweet girl and she's lucky to have a friend like you.'

'I'm lucky to have a friend like her,' I said.

We chatted some more, and then I noticed that

Mam had a huge smile on her face.

'I have a big surprise for you too, pet,' she said. 'I was trying to save it until you were ready to go back to Lissadell, but I can't wait any more.'

'What is it?' I asked. Mam didn't have money to buy anything extra for me, so I was a bit confused.

'It's a letter,' she said. 'All the way from America!'

Now I felt like jumping up and down even though I'm supposed to be much too grown up for that. Hanora had gone to America just after Christmas, and since then I'd had no news of her.

Mam took the letter from the safe ledge where she put all important things.

I turned it over and over in my hands, looking at the familiar handwriting, remembering how Hanora and I had sat together on our first day of school, struggling to form letters with our babyish hands.

Even the return address on the back of the envelope was exciting – 307B East 154th St, New York City.

I carefully opened the envelope. The paper inside was fine and light, and the writing covered both sides. I read slowly, savouring each word my friend had sent me from the other side of the world. As I read, I could hear her voice in my head, and the loneliness of it all brought tears to my eyes.

Dearest Lily,

I have so much to tell you, one letter won't be enough, but I'll do my best.

New York is so big, you wouldn't believe it if you could see it. The buildings are bigger than you could imagine, and the streets are full of motor cars and bicycles and people rushing everywhere. It's always loud here even in the middle of the night.

Sometimes it seems as if the whole world wants to live in America. Every day new families come from Italy and Greece. Everyone is so dark and so handsome, and I love listening to them talking so fast in their funny languages. There was a nice family from Russia here for a while,

but they all moved to Detroit when they heard that Ford Motors had doubled the rates of pay. Now workers there get 5 whole dollars a day! (You mightn't know what dollars are, but trust me, Lily, that's a lot of money.)

I'm living in a boarding house with my sisters. We have a nice, clean, big room, and the landlady isn't too strict. My brothers are living nearby, but Seamus is sweet on a girl from Chicago and I think they might get engaged soon. Mam and Dad will go mad when they hear because they still hope he's going to go home and marry Mary Carty. I have a job in a factory where we make mens' shirts. It's not a very good job, but I'm hoping to get something better soon. We have a half day on Saturday and all of Sunday off. On Sundays me and my sisters usually put on our best dresses and go for a walk in Central Park. In January it was so cold I thought I would die.

Oh, Lily, I like it here, but sometimes I cry for Mam and Dad and my old life in Sligo.

I miss the happy days at school with you and Rose and the Master – that all seems very distant now.

Please write back to me at the address on the envelope.
I want to hear all about Lissadell and Nellie and Maeve.
Your dear friend
Hanora.

I folded the envelope, and wiped away a tear.

'Is Hanora keeping well?' asked Mam.

'Yes, it sounds as if she is, but ...' I couldn't say any more for fear of crying my eyes out. Mam put her arms around me. 'I understand, pet,' she said. 'I understand.'

Chapter Five

I'm sure the Gore-Booths were having a lovely relaxing holiday, but by the third week I was fit to die. My arms ached from scrubbing and when I walked I was bent over like an old woman of fifty.

Nellie and I were in the china room, and we had taken down every single piece of china, and cleaned the shelves and lined them with fresh white paper. Nellie hummed as she worked, while I distracted myself by thinking of the beach on a sunny day. Just as we were putting the last of the huge gravy jugs back in place, Mrs Bailey came in. As usual she was carrying a long piece of paper with a list of jobs for Nellie and me to do.

'Tomorrow is Thursday,' she said to Nellie, as if that might be news to her. Thursday was Nellie's day off, and I wished it was mine too. I didn't know if I'd

last until Saturday.

'Yes, Mrs Bailey,' said Nellie politely.

'I was thinking that this week it would be best if you took your day off on Saturday, the same as Lily. That way the two of you can work together on the last of the big jobs tomorrow and on Friday – far more efficient all around.'

'Yes, Mrs Bailey,' said Nellie.

'Very well,' said Mrs Bailey. 'Now off you go. Time for you to get started on Mr Kilgallon's office.'

As Mrs Bailey hurried along the corridor, I stared at Nellie.

'That's not right,' I said. 'Thursday is always your day off. She can't change it like that, can she?'

'It doesn't matter,' said Nellie. 'I didn't have any big arrangements for tomorrow. I was only going to practise my reading and go for a walk and mend my grey dress. I can do all of that just as easily on Saturday. Now come along, or we'll be in trouble with Mrs Bailey.'

Just then Mrs Bailey turned around and walked back towards us.

'Oh no,' I whispered. 'I'll fall down and die if she's thought of another job for us to do.'

But Mrs Bailey wasn't even looking at her list.

'I nearly forgot,' she said with a big smile on her face. 'I should have mentioned that you two girls have done very good work these past few weeks – very good work indeed. The family return on Monday night, and at this rate it's looking as if all of your work will be finished by Friday evening.'

Now I smiled too. I had been wondering if our jobs would ever be done.

'So,' continued Mrs Bailey. 'I don't see any reason why you can't both have a day off on Sunday too – as a reward for all your hard work. What do you think of that?'

What did I think of that?

With two days off, I could spend the night at home with my family, sleeping in my own bed, just like I'd

done for most of my life!

I wanted to kiss and hug Mrs Bailey until she begged for mercy.

But I knew that would not have been a good idea, so I hugged Nellie instead.

'Thank you, Mrs Bailey,' we said together.

Mrs Bailey laughed. 'You're good girls, both of you,' she said. 'Now hurry along with your work, before I change my mind.'

* * *

On Saturday morning I was so excited I thought I would burst. Nellie lay in bed and watched as I ran around our little room, selecting the things I'd need – my nightgown and my lovely doll Julianne, who I often brought home so Winnie and Anne could play with her.

'It will be such a surprise for Mam when she hears I can stay for the night,' I said. 'It's months since I've

done that.'

'I'm happy for you, Lily,' said Nellie. 'You've been working so hard, you deserve a treat.'

'But you've been working hard too,' I said, feeling guilty. 'Just as hard as me. What treat will you get?'

She smiled. 'Not working is a big treat for me. I can stay in bed as long as I want, and relax and read and ...'

And then I had a wonderful idea. 'Come with me.'

'Pardon?' She looked at me as if she didn't understand my words.

'Come with me,' I said again.

'Oh! You mean, walk a bit of the road with you, and keep you company – is that it? Yes, I'll do that if you like,' she said, jumping out of bed. 'Give me a minute to get dressed.'

'Oh, Nellie. That's not what I'm saying at all. I want you to come with me, and finally meet Mam and the little ones, and have dinner and tea with us, and stay for the night – and everything.'

Nellie's whole face lit up as if the sun were shining on it – though there was no sun coming through our little basement window.

'That would be so ...' she began, and then she continued. 'But no. I couldn't do that. It's not fair. You want your time with your family, and what would your mam say, and Mrs Bailey? It's very nice of you to offer Lily, but I think it's best if I stay here.'

I wanted to shake her. Why did this lovely girl always feel as if she didn't deserve to be happy?

Suddenly I knew the answer to this. It was because she'd had so few nice things in her life. Every day I understood more about why she had been so sullen and cross when I first met her.

'I'll talk to Mrs Bailey,' I said. 'She was so happy when we finished all the cleaning yesterday, I know she won't mind. And Mam is always saying that she'd love to meet you, and we've got lots of room – well not exactly lots – but there's always room for one more. Please say you'll come. Please?'

And now her face lit up again. 'If you're sure?'

'I'm very sure. Now hurry up. Let's not waste a single moment of this special day.'

* * *

The walk back home always seemed to take ages, but with Nellie by my side the time flew by.

'Not much further,' I said. 'Just around this bend and we're there.'

Nellie stopped walking. 'If you've changed your mind, I can go back to Lissadell,' she said. 'I know the way now.'

'You're coming with me,' I said. 'We agreed, and it's going to be lovely.'

She started walking and then stopped again. 'I should have brought a present for your mam.'

Poor Nellie had so little, I didn't know what kind of a present she could have brought.

'I've got a *huge* basket of food from Cook,' I said.

'We don't need to bring anything else.'

Without another word Nellie turned and ran back the way we had come. I wanted to cry. She was always so kind to me – why wouldn't she let me share something nice with her?

But then she stopped and called over her shoulder. 'Just wait one minute,' she said. 'I saw some beautiful wild flowers here – I'll pick them for your mam.'

I smiled. 'Mam loves flowers – and I know she's going to love you too.'

* * *

We stopped when we got to the door of my mam's little house. Nellie looked as if she were about ready to fall into a faint, so I took her hand and squeezed it, trying to make her feel better

Inside I could hear the boys practising their spelling, and Winnie and Anne chatting over one of their made-up games. This was always a strange moment

for me – the moment I realised that when I was at Lissadell, life at home went on perfectly well without me.

I was just about to go in when I remembered something important.

'Don't say anything about Maeve,' I whispered. 'Mam doesn't know I'm friends with her. She wouldn't understand, and she'd worry about me.'

'Don't worry,' said Nellie. 'I won't say a word. You can trust ...'

Just then the door flew open and Mam was there, giving us her lovely warm smile. 'My darling girl,' she said when she'd finished hugging me. 'I thought I heard footsteps. And who is this lovely young lady with you?'

Poor Nellie's face turned bright red, but she looked very pleased. I wondered if anyone had ever called her a young lady before.

'This is my friend Nellie,' I said.

'Nellie!' said Mam. 'Lily has told us all about you,

and I'm so happy to finally meet you.'

'Hello,' said Nellie, shyly, holding out the bunch of flowers and leaves that she'd arranged to look very pretty.

'Thank you so much,' said Mam. 'They are only perfect. Now come in the two of you and have a glass of water. You must be tired after your walk.'

I smiled at Nellie as we followed Mam inside, and I knew everything was going to be just right.

Chapter Six

The rest of the day was simply lovely. After ten minutes of pretend-shyness, Winnie and Anne were hanging on to Nellie's dress and asking her to sing for them, and Mam chatted away easily as if she had known her all her life. Denis and Jimmy showed her their collection of dried conkers.

'Conkers are pretty,' said Nellie. 'I like seeing them on the ground in autumn – but why have you saved them? What are they for?'

'*Everyone* knows what you do with conkers,' said Jimmy.

'Didn't you play conkers at school?' asked Denis.

'No,' said Nellie.

I suppose her school in the workhouse was a bit different to the one in the village where I used to go. I worried that Denis and Jimmy were going to

ask stupid questions and make things awkward, but I should have trusted my little brothers.

'It's easy,' said Denis. 'First you make a hole in the conker – but you have to be careful. I got a fierce bad cut doing it last year.'

'And you put it on a string,' said Jimmy.

And then the two of them spent about half an hour explaining all the rules and regulations of a game of conkers, before Mam rescued Nellie by asking for help with peeling the potatoes for dinner.

At dinner and tea-time, though Mam's food was plainer than anything at Lissadell House, Nellie praised it as if it were fit for the finest ladies and gentlemen.

When it began to get dark, Mam lit the candles and we all chatted, with Winnie in my arms, and Anne cuddled up on Nellie's lap. After a while I noticed that Winnie had stopped twiddling my hair.

'Is she asleep,' I whispered to Jimmy who was on the stool beside us.

'Sound asleep,' he said.

I loved holding her, but soon my arms began to go numb from the weight of my little sister.

'I think it might be time for bed,' said Mam when she saw how uncomfortable I was.

She was right, but now I felt embarrassed. I knew Nellie had once lived in a workhouse, but that was ages ago. Nowadays she was used to the luxury of the servants' quarters at Lissadell. She was used to a bedroom with a fireplace and a gas light. She was used to a bed all to herself.

What was she going to say when she saw how my family slept?

Would she laugh when she saw that I had to share a bed with all of my brothers and sisters?

And where on earth was *she* going to sleep?

Why hadn't I thought about all of this before I invited her to stay?

But I should have known that I could trust Mam to make everything work. As soon as Nellie and I

had carried Winnie and Anne into bed, and kissed them good night, Mam chased the boys to bed too and tucked them in. Then she gave a big yawn. 'You know, I'm so tired I think I'll sleep in here with the children,' she said. 'Move over there and make room for your mam.'

They did as they were told, and Mam climbed in beside them, pulling the blankets over her.

'Lily, why don't you and Nellie sleep in my bed?' she asked.

'Are you sure?' said Nellie to Mam. 'I don't want to put you out. I can easily sleep on the floor with my coat over me. I don't mind at—'

Instead of answering, Mam gave a big loud snore. I giggled. I know Mam so well, and understood that she was pretending, but Nellie didn't notice.

'Your poor mam must be very tired,' she whispered. 'Let's go to bed so we don't disturb her any more.'

So I led the way to Mam's bed in the kitchen, and my friend and I settled down for the night.

* * *

In the morning, as it was Sunday, we had milk in our porridge. After breakfast, Mam tidied up, while Nellie and I played with the little girls.

'You should go and see Rose,' said Mam as she dried her hands. 'She'll be home with her family for the day.'

'Oh,' I said. 'I don't know. Maybe she ...'

I wasn't sure what to do. Rose was one of my best friends from school. Now she worked in her uncle's shop in Sligo, and only came home on Sundays, while I was usually only at home on Saturdays – so I hadn't seen her for many months. Our lives were so different these days.

What would we say to each other?

Would we still be friends?

What would she think of Nellie?

What would Nellie think of her?

'Rose!' said Nellie then. 'Your friend Rose is at

home? You've told me so much about her, Lily, I'd love to meet her.'

Mam laughed. 'I think that's decided then,' she said. 'Off you go, and I'll see you soon.'

The short walk to Rose's house took a long time as everyone stopped to say hello, and to be introduced to my friend from Lissadell. Ours was a quiet village and a new person always stood out. Mrs Carty wanted to touch Nellie's 'glorious red hair', and Old William said we could go and see his goats later if we wanted.

'Everyone here is so nice and friendly,' said Nellie.

'I suppose they are,' I said. She was right, except I'd never noticed before. Home is home, and I'd never thought about it very much.

I felt nervous when I got to Rose's house. Should I knock on the door, or just let myself in, the way I used to when we were school-friends? In the end I didn't have to make a decision, as Rose looked out the window and saw us.

A second later she was holding my hand, and talking at a hundred miles an hour.

'Slow down,' I said laughing. 'I know we've got months to catch up on, but I can't understand a word you're saying.'

Then Rose saw Nellie.

'I'm Rose,' she said, holding out her hand.

'Nellie,' said Nellie a little shyly.

They smiled at each other and I knew I shouldn't have worried.

The three of us walked through the fields until dinnertime. Rose talked about her job in Sligo, and Nellie and I talked about Lissadell, and we laughed a lot, and everything was lovely.

* * *

Much too soon it was time for Nellie and me to start our walk back to Lissadell. Nellie thanked Mam a hundred times, making her laugh.

'It was lovely to meet you,' Nellie,' she said. 'And I know you don't usually get Saturdays off, but when you do, please come and see us again.'

'I'd like that,' said Nellie shyly.

Winnie and Anne clung on to both of us, begging for kisses and hugs. Mam gave me a warm goodbye hug, and then gave Nellie one too. I didn't mind – I'm used to sharing my mam, and I know she's got enough love for all of us – and Nellie too.

* * *

As we walked, Nellie was very quiet – even quieter than usual. Maybe she hadn't liked my home, or my mam or my brothers and sisters? Maybe she was sorry she hadn't stayed at Lissadell reading and doing her jobs?

'Is everything all right, Nellie?' I asked.

She nodded, but didn't answer.

'Are you cross because Denis and Jimmy laughed

at you over the conkers? Or did Winnie and Anne annoy you with all their questions and chatter? Did Mam say something that offended you?'

Now she shook her head and began to walk a little faster.

'Oh, Nellie,' I said. 'Why won't you talk to me? What's wrong? Please tell me what's wrong.'

At last she stopped walking. 'Everything is fine,' she said. 'Everyone in your family is lovely, and they were very kind to me. I'm a bit tired is all that's wrong. You kicked me a lot in the night, so I didn't sleep very well.'

'I'm so glad that's the only thing – and I'm sorry about the kicking. I'm not used to sharing a bed any-more.'

'That's all right,' she said. 'Now let's get going. The Gore-Booths are back tomorrow and we will have an early start getting ready for them.'

* * *

A cramp in my leg woke me in the middle of the night. As I stretched it out, the way my Granny once showed me, I heard a small noise from Nellie's bed.

'Nellie?' I whispered. 'Are you awake?'

She didn't answer, so I told myself I'd imagined it as I rubbed my sore leg, and tried to get back to sleep.

Then the sound came again, and this time I understood what it was. It was the sound of someone trying to cry without being heard.

'Nellie,' I whispered as I jumped out of bed. 'What is it?'

I sat on the edge of her bed and stroked her hair, and jumped when I realised that her pillow was soaking wet.

She sat up, threw her arms around me, and sobbed for a long time. I hugged her and stroked her back and waited. In the end, when her sobs were a little less, I let her go.

'Please, Nellie,' I said. 'Tell me what's wrong. Tell me how I can help you.'

'*No one* can help me,' she said. 'No one.'

'Then tell me anyway. Mam always says that a trouble shared is a trouble halved.'

I thought Mam's words were true, but they made Nellie cry even more.

'Oh, Lily,' she sobbed. 'That's it. You've got your mam to tell you wise things, and you see her every week and love her and … you have your brothers and sisters – and they are such darlings – and your friends and your neighbours … and you've got a home and a village and a place to go where everyone knows you and everyone loves you … and sometimes I get so lonely.'

I held her hand as I started to cry too. 'Nellie, I'm so sorry. I shouldn't have brought you home with me. I was trying to do a nice thing, and all I've done is make you sad.'

'It's not your fault. You are always so kind to me. I'm often sad, but I try not to show it.'

How could I have forgotten what Nellie was like

when I first met her? She never smiled or laughed, and when I tried to be friends with her she pushed me away. It took me a long time to understand that after losing her parents and her sisters and her friends, she was afraid to let herself be close to anyone. She was afraid of getting hurt.

'You can come home with me again,' I said. 'Mam would love to see you. The next time you have a Saturday ... I stopped talking. It could be a whole year before Nellie got a Saturday off again, and how could she last all those weeks and months with nothing else to look forward to?

'I know I'm lucky Lady Mary rescued me from the workhouse,' she said. 'I know I'm lucky to be working here, but ...'

'But what?'

'Lissadell is all I have. If I lost my job and had to leave here, what would I do? Even the workhouse probably wouldn't take me back. I'd have nowhere to go, no one to go to.'

It all sounded so hopeless, I didn't know what to say. When Winnie and Anne cried I could always find a way to make them feel better – a joke or a tickle, or a treat or a promise – but what could I do for Nellie?

'I will always be your friend,' I said. 'Always and forever.'

She squeezed my hand a little tighter, but she didn't say anything.

'Maybe, one day,' I said. 'Maybe one day your sisters …'

I knew Nellie had two sisters, but she never talked about them, and when I mentioned them she always changed the subject quickly. Now, for the first time ever, she told me a little more. 'Before she got sick, my sister Lizzie was so lively and full of fun. The two of us were always laughing and making mischief.'

The Nellie I knew was serious and hard-working and obedient. She always followed the rules and tried her hardest to be the best housemaid a girl could be.

It was difficult to imagine her making mischief of any kind at all. What terrible things had happened to make her change her so much?

'Lizzie was often in trouble,' she continued. 'But no one could be cross with her for long. Daddy said she had a smile that was like a ray of sunshine on a cloudy day.'

'She sounds nice – and what about your other sister?'

'Johanna was the oldest, and always a bit more serious than Lizzie and me. Mam said her job was to take care of us and keep us safe. She helped to mind us when Mam was busy, and then ... when ... Mam and Dad got sick, Johanna looked after all of us. Lizzie and I tried to help, but we were only little, and then, when ...' She started to cry again.

'It's all right if you don't want to talk about this,' I said.

She wiped her eyes with the sleeve of her night-gown. 'You're my friend,' she said. 'I want to tell you.

When Mam and Daddy died, Johanna tried to keep us three girls together. We were sick and cold and hungry all the time, but she did her best. The neighbours gave us food sometimes, but they were poor too, and didn't have much to share. Sometimes I cried and cried for Mam, and Johanna would cuddle me and sing to me. She'd stroke my hair and sing an old Irish song she learned from our granny. In the end, the words would soothe me and I'd fall asleep in her arms, and then I'd wake up and Mam and Daddy would still be gone, and I'd cry and cry some more. And then the neighbours took us to the workhouse.'

'How *could* they do that to you?'

'It was probably for the best. The workhouse was awful, but if we weren't there we would have starved to death. We were so scared, but Johanna said we had to be brave. When we got there, a woman took me into a room and washed me and cut my hair. I screamed when I saw it on the ground, and she slapped me and told me to shut my mouth. When she brought me

out of the room … Lizzie and Johanna were gone –
and I never saw them again. I cried for them, but no
one listened. Later I learned that the workhouse was
divided into different sections.'

'I don't understand.'

'There were sections for men, and women, and
children of different ages, and for sick people. There
were huge high walls between the sections, and even
if we could have climbed them, no one would have
dared. Oh, Lily, how I'd love to see my dear sisters
again!'

'Maybe you will.'

She shook her head. 'They are most likely dead.
There was terrible fever in the workhouse and so
many died … and poor Lizzie was sick before she
even got there, and Johanna was so thin and pale …'

'But you don't know for sure.'

'I'm their little sister. If they were alive, they would
have come to find me. Johanna was like a mam to me
in the end. She would never forget me.'

And then I understood that there was nothing I could say. Some things can't be fixed. All I could do was hold my friend and stroke her hair, and so that's what I did.

After a while, Nellie shivered.

'Look at you,' I said. 'You're frozen half to death. You need to get back into bed.' Then I remembered the damp pillow, and realised that her sheet was probably wet too.

'Come,' I said. 'You can sleep in my bed with me tonight.'

She was like a little child as she let me lead her to my bed and cover her with my blanket. I wrapped Mam's shawl over her shoulders and then I jumped in beside her and snuggled up close.

'Thank you, Lily,' she said. 'I feel a little better now.'

'I'm glad – and there's one more thing.'

'What?'

'If I kick you in my sleep, you can kick me back. All right?'

'I will.'

'Promise?'

'I promise.'

I could tell she was smiling so I closed my eyes and went to sleep.

Chapter Seven

a few days later Mrs Bailey sent me to the flower garden. As I walked back with an armful of flowers for the dining room, I deliberately walked slowly, enjoying the sunshine and the breeze and the birdsong and the crisp crunch of my boots on the gravel.

Suddenly the peace was shattered with a loud shout. 'Lily! Watch out! Get off the path or ... oh, no!'

I jumped off the path just as Maeve came up behind me on a bicycle that looked much too big for her. She swerved and skidded and I was showered with gravel as she fell off the path and on to the grass beside me. I dropped my flowers and went to her, keeping well clear of the still-spinning bicycle wheels.

'Maeve, are you all right? Did you hurt yourself?'

She jumped up, laughing. 'That was a close one. I

thought I had the hang of it, but maybe I need a little more practice.'

'You've cut yourself. Look.'

'It's only a scratch,' she said, ignoring the blood that was trickling down her arm.

Mr Kilgallon once said that Maeve's mother, Countess Markievicz, was the bravest child he had ever seen. I think Maeve was a little like her mother in this.

'And look at your skirt,' I said, pointing to where it was torn and grass-stained. 'It's ruined.'

'So it is,' she said, as if this meant nothing. But why would it matter to her, when she had wardrobes full of clothes both at Lissadell and Ardeevin?

'Where on earth did the bike come from?' I asked.

'Uncle Joss bought it for Aunt Mary, but she thinks cycling is unladylike. She said she'd rather die than be seen on a bike, so I'm allowed to have it.'

'And don't *you* think it is unladylike?'

She laughed. 'Definitely not. Did you know my

mother spent part of her honeymoon cycling in France?'

'No, I didn't know that.'

'Well she did – and she said it was a lot of fun. Do you want to have a go?'

'I'd like that very much,' I said. 'But Mrs Bailey is waiting for these flowers.'

'I'll give them to her,' she said. 'And I'll tell her I need you to help with my cycling practice.'

Before I could argue, she had gathered up most of the flowers and raced away. While she was gone, I examined the bike – I'd never seen one up so close before. It was black and shiny with a lovely leather saddle, and a pretty wicker basket strapped on to the handlebars.

'Mrs Bailey said we've got an hour,' said Maeve when she came back. 'So we'd better make it count. Let's go to the coach house courtyard – maybe cycling on gravel can wait for lesson two.'

* * *

It was scary at first but such fun! Maeve was very patient as she followed me up and down the court-yard, rescuing me when I was wobbling, and praising me whenever I managed to go in a straight line for more than a second or two.

'You're a natural,' she said, sounding a bit surprised.

I smiled. Maybe carrying all those buckets of coal up the back stairs had improved my balance.

'Actually you're much better than I was when I started,' she said.

She had only started an hour before me, and now she was acting as if she were an expert, but I didn't say this – I was trying too hard not to end up in a heap on the ground!

* * *

Before long we were both able to cycle perfectly well

and we stopped for a rest.

'I've had the most marvellous idea,' said Maeve.

I wasn't sure I liked the sound of that. Maeve's marvellous ideas usually involved me breaking lots of rules.

'Why don't you use the bicycle to go home on Saturdays?' she said. 'It would be much quicker than walking, and you'd have all that extra time with your family.'

'Oh, Maeve. Do you really think I could?'

As soon as the words were out of my mouth I thought of all kinds of reasons it wouldn't work.

'What would Lady Mary say? What if you want to use the bicycle? What if something happens to it?'

'Lady Mary won't care – she doesn't want to ever see it again. And I'll most likely be at Ardeevin and the bicycle will be gathering dust in the coach house. And if something happens to it, Albert will be able to fix it. And you can use the basket on the front to carry treats for your family. Oh, do say you'll use the

bicycle, Lily. Please do.'

I laughed. 'All right,' I said. 'I'll use it. Thank you Maeve.'

When it was time for me to go back to work, we took the bicycle back to the coach house.

'This is where it's kept,' said Maeve, as she propped it against a wall. 'You can come and borrow it any time you wish.'

Already I felt excited. What would my family say when they saw me on a bicycle?

* * *

As we walked back towards the main house Maeve asked if I had a nice time while she was away in England.

'Yes, it was nice enough,' I said, smiling to myself. Maeve had no idea how hard we servants had to work while she and her family were away.

'And how is your mother and the rest of the family?'

I didn't answer. Nowadays, even having a family made me feel guilty, because poor Nellie was so alone in the world.

Maeve noticed my silence. 'Is everything all right? Is someone sick?'

'No. It's just that ...'

And then, all in a rush I told Maeve how Nellie had visited my family, and how upset she was afterwards.

'Poor Nellie,' she said. 'How sad for her.'

'I wish I could help her somehow, but I don't know what to do. Her sisters are my only hope, but how could I find out where they are, or even if they are alive?'

'You could borrow the bicycle and go to the workhouse and ask them?'

Suddenly I got a small picture of what it was like to be Maeve – what it was like to grow up without fear of the workhouse. What it was like not to be terrified every time your mam or dad coughed, that

they would get sick, and that the workhouse would be your only future.

'Maybe I could do that,' I said slowly. But I knew I was being stupid. Even if I did the bravest thing of my whole life, I knew no one would tell me anything. They would laugh – or decide I was destitute, and drag me in and make me stay.

'No,' I said. 'I couldn't do that. There's lots of work-houses, so I wouldn't even know which one to go to. And I'd be too afraid, and they wouldn't tell me any-thing anyway.'

'I wouldn't be afraid,' said Maeve. 'But I suppose they wouldn't tell me anything either.'

'So how can we ...?'

'How did Nellie get out of the workhouse? How did she end up here? Who ...?'

And as she said the words, I knew what I had to do. 'Lady Mary helped her,' I said. 'Lady Mary went to the workhouse and saved her.'

'So that means ...'

'Yes! Lady Mary will be able to find out about Nellie's sisters. Why didn't I think of that before? Do you think I could ask her? Do you think she might help?'

'I'm sure she would be happy to help. I can go and talk to her now if you like.'

I liked the idea of that very much. Even though Lady Mary was always kind to me, I couldn't help being a little bit afraid of her.

'Yes, if you ...' But before I could finish the sentence, Sir Josslyn's car came along the drive towards us, and Maeve's granny was leaning out of the window looking very cross.

'Maeve Alyss,' she said. 'Look at the state of you! Come along, climb in, it's time for us to go home. Miss Clayton has big plans for you this evening.'

Maeve made a face at me, and then turned and smiled at her grandmother. 'Sorry, Gaga,' she said.

'When will you be back at Lissadell?' I whispered.

'I don't know,' said Maeve. 'It could be ages. I'm sorry.'

Then she climbed into the car and was gone.

* * *

'At last!' said Mrs Bailey when she saw me. 'Hurry along and tidy up the drawing room.'

I was turning to do as she said, when I realised it was time for me to be brave. Mam says patience is a virtue, but I wasn't so sure. What if I was sitting in a corner being patient, and Nellie's sisters were never found at all?

'I'm sorry, Mrs Bailey,' I said. 'I will do the drawing room very soon, but first ... first there's something important I have to say to Lady Mary.'

Mrs Bailey looked ready to explode. 'You certainly may not go annoying Lady Mary,' she said. 'If there is a message for her, you may pass it on to me, and I will relay it when I see her in the morning – *if* I think it is appropriate.'

Mrs Bailey could be very kind, but I wasn't sure she

would understand what I wanted to ask, and why it was suddenly so urgent.

'Maeve asked me to bring the message to Lady Mary,' I said (which was sort of the truth.) 'She won't be very pleased if I don't do as she asked.'

Mrs Bailey did not look happy. It must have been hard living in a world where a young girl like Maeve was seen to be more important than a grown-up like her.

'Very well,' she said. 'Lady Mary is in the bow drawing room. Give her your message and come directly back here, do you understand?'

'Yes, Mrs Bailey,' I said as I ran off.

* * *

'Come in.' Even with those two words, I could recognise Lady Mary's sweet voice.

As I closed the door behind me, I was glad to see that she was on her own. If Sir Josslyn had been with

her I think I might have curled up and died on the spot.

'What can I do for you, Lily?' she asked.

'It's about Nellie,' I said.

Lady Mary looked surprised. 'If something is wrong with Nellie, then you must speak to Mrs Bailey about it. You really should understand how things work by now.'

I could feel my face going red. Why did this house have to have so many rules? Why did I always seem to be breaking them?

'I'm sorry, Lady Mary. It's … you see … Mrs Bailey couldn't … you're the only … poor Nellie …'

Tears came to my eyes and I couldn't finish.

'Now, Lily, don't fret,' she said gently. 'Tell me what is wrong and I'll see if I can help. Is Nellie unwell in some way?'

'No. She's not unwell, only ….'

'Only what?'

Lady Mary listened patiently as I rushed out

my story.

'The poor little girl,' she said when had I finished, and was standing still with my hands clasped in front of me, the way Mrs Bailey had taught me. I thought I could see tears in Lady Mary's eyes.

'I love to see my own little ones play together,' she said. 'And I cannot imagine the cruelty of someone who would see fit to tear them away from each other. Those workhouses ….' She stopped and wiped away a tear with a lace-trimmed handkerchief. 'Those workhouses should not be allowed to do this.'

I agreed with her, but I didn't say anything. A housemaid like me couldn't change the world – all I wanted to do was make it a little better for my friend.

Lady Mary put her handkerchief away and began to write in the notebook that was on the table in front of her.

'It is very kind of you to care for your friend like this, Lily,' she said. 'But now you may leave it with me. I will make enquiries about Nellie's sisters

immediately. If it is necessary to visit the workhouse, then I will do that. I promise I will do everything I can to find out what happened to those two poor girls.'

I thanked her and ran from the room – and all that afternoon, as I worked, I wondered if I had done the right thing at all.

Chapter Eight

For the next few days, I worked as if I were in a trance. As Nellie and I blackleaded the grates, and lit the many fires and lay out towels in the dressing rooms, and made the beds, and swept and polished and scrubbed, all I wanted to do was to wrap my arms around her and protect her from the world.

What if Lady Mary discovered that Nellie's sisters had died?

Would it be right to tell Nellie, or would it be better to protect her from the truth?

What if I had taken away the last tiny bit of hope she had left?

How could I call myself her friend if I had done that?

A few times I saw Lady Mary from a distance, but she didn't notice me, and she never came near.

Sometimes I was desperate to know the truth. At other times I wished I had kept my stupid mouth shut.

*　*　*

One day, just as we finishing our dinner, Michael, the oldest of the Gore-Booth children came running into the dining hall. He was breathless, and worried-looking and the front of his coat was wet and sandy. Michael was a serious little boy, who rarely came near the servants' quarters. He stopped when he saw that the room was full of people, and then he said in a small voice. 'Can someone come and help me please? It's sort of an emergency.'

Mr Kilgallon and Mrs Bailey and two of the footmen got to their feet, and now Michael looked even more worried.

'It's not a huge big emergency,' he said. 'Nobody is sick or dead or anything like that.'

Everyone sat down again, and Mrs Bailey turned to Nellie and me. 'Could you two girls go and see what is the matter?'

Nellie and I followed Michael along the servants' corridor to the back door. He led us into the small courtyard, and pointed at the little stone pond in the corner.

'Oh,' said Nellie and I together as we saw the small grey creature with the huge eyes.

'It's a baby seal,' said Michael proudly. 'He was all on his own on the beach with no Mummy or Daddy or anything, and I saved him and I carried him all the way back by myself.'

'He looks very big for you to carry,' I said.

Michael put his head down. 'I carried him a small little bit and then a gardening man helped me,' he said.

'Were you on the beach by yourself?' I asked, wondering if Isabelle or one of the other children's maids was going to be in big trouble.

'I'm not allowed to go anywhere by myself, but I should be, because I'm five and a half,' he said. 'Nurse was with me, but she was cross when I said I wanted to save the seal. When we got to here the gardening man went back to work. Nurse said she had to bath Brian, and I should ask a servant to help me, so that's what I did.'

I smiled. Everyone knew that Nurse was terrified of animals, and had once run up the stairs screaming when a puppy tried to lick her leg.

The pond was small, but the seal looked happy enough flopping around in the water.

'What do you want us to do?' asked Nellie.

'He's hungry,' said Michael. 'Can you get him some food?'

'Of course we will,' I said. 'You wait here and Nellie and I will find something for him.

No one was sure what seal pups ate, but in the end, Cook gave us a very small fish, and some warm milk in a bottle that had once been used to feed an

orphaned lamb.

Michael took the fish, and held it towards the seal, who sniffed it for a second, and then swallowed it whole, making Michael laugh. Then he held out the bottle, but the seal looked confused.

'He doesn't know it's milk,' I said. 'Try splashing some on his nose, so he understands.'

Michael did as I suggested. The seal blinked in surprise, and then as a few drops dripped down his nose, he stuck out his tiny pink tongue and began to lick them.

'Quick,' said Nellie. 'Give him the bottle, before he changes his mind.'

Michael jabbed the bottle towards him, and after a second the pup began to suck.

A huge smile came across Michael's face, as he held the bottle carefully. 'He's the cleverest seal in the whole world,' he said. 'He's called Spotty, and he's all mine and no one else's, so you can go and do your work now and I will mind him.'

Nellie and I looked at each other, not sure if we should leave him, but then Isabelle appeared.

'What a little pet,' she said to Michael. 'Aren't you the clever boy to save him?'

Then she turned to Nellie and me. 'I'll mind him now,' she said. 'Mrs Bailey says you're to go inside and get started on cleaning the silver.'

I sighed. Why did my life have to be so boring?

* * *

On Saturday Nellie and I got up early as usual. She dressed in her uniform, while I put on my dress, ready for the journey home.

'Please tell your mam and the boys I say hello,' said Nellie as I laced up my boots. 'And give your gorgeous little sisters a big kiss and a hug from me.'

I smiled at her. A few times I had tried to talk to her about the night she had cried in my arms, but she always pushed me away.

'I was being silly,' she would say. 'Forget it ever happened. I was making a fuss about nothing.'

It definitely wasn't nothing, but if she didn't want to talk about it, what could I do?

'Nellie, I wish you could come with me,' I said now.

'That's all right. I have plenty to occupy me here. Are you excited about the journey?'

'What do you mean?'

'You said Miss Maeve is letting you use her bicycle.'

I hadn't seen Maeve since the day we had both learned to cycle, and I had *completely* forgotten that she had said I could use the bicycle.

'She did say that,' I said. 'But I don't know if I dare to.'

'You have to take it,' said Nellie. 'Imagine all the extra time you can have with your family.'

'You're right,' I said. 'Wish me luck.'

* * *

Albert was working on the engine of the motor car when I got to the coach house.

He was the first person I met on my very first day at Lissadell, and he had always been kind to me. Still, I felt nervous as I went over to the bicycle. What if he didn't believe that I was allowed to take it?

'Miss Maeve said I can borrow her bicycle to go and see my family,' I said shyly. 'Do you think that is all right?'

'I think that is a wonderful idea,' said Albert. 'Here, let me help you.'

He wiped his oily hands on a rag and wheeled the bike outside for me. He helped me to arrange Cook's basket inside the larger bicycle basket, and then he held the bicycle as I got on and tried to remember how cycling was done.

'Off you go,' he said, giving me a little push.

I squealed as I wobbled and swayed and very nearly crashed into a huge stone pot of flowers. I somehow stayed upright, found my balance and began to pedal.

Albert clapped his hands, but I didn't dare to look back at him.

'Have a lovely time,' he called.

'Thank you,' I called back, but I was already so far away, I wasn't sure he could hear me.

* * *

I was feeling very confident by the time I had left the estate, and was on the open road. It was starting to rain a little, but I didn't care. I felt like the queen of the road as I raced along, with my skirt flapping madly and the breeze blowing my hair out behind me. In no time at all I was nearly home.

Denis and Jimmy were standing outside their friend Brendan's house as I came by. They stared at me the way you stare at a stranger in a small, quiet village. I smiled when I realised that they didn't recognise me. I had nearly made it past them, when Brendan let out a big shout.

'That's your sister, boys,' he said. 'That's Lily.'

I watched as my brothers looked doubtful at first, and then began to laugh.

'Lily,' they called as I sailed past them. 'Give us a go. Come on, give us a go.'

'Sorry, I can't,' I said. 'I'm not allowed.'

I cycled on through the village, and while I didn't dare to look over my shoulder, I knew the boys were running after me. Soon, I could tell by the shouts that they had been joined by some of their friends.

When I finally stopped at my own house, I turned back to see what looked like every child in the village running along, cheering and laughing and pointing at me. As they came close, they pushed and shoved, all trying to touch the bike and ring the bell.

Mam's friend, Molly Carty, came along. 'Well look at you, Lily,' she said. 'All fancy on your bike, like the Queen of Sheba, or maybe even the Countess Markievicz herself.'

Just then Mam came out of the house – I suppose

all the noise made her think there was an army going past. When she saw me and the bicycle and Molly Carty, her face went pink. Mam always hates a fuss.

'Lily, child,' she said. 'Come in out of it.' Before I could argue, she had grabbed the bicycle, and was wheeling it through the door, and propping it up against the kitchen wall. 'I think this will be safer in here.'

Denis and Jimmy followed us inside, happy to be part of the excitement, and enjoying the jealous looks of their friends. Molly tried to come in too, but Mam blocked her way.

'I'm sorry, Molly,' she said firmly. 'Lily and I have a lot to talk about, so it's best if we don't have any visitors for a little while.'

Molly tossed her head. 'I was only being neigh-bourly,' she said as she walked away. I looked at Mam to see if she was cross, but she was only laughing, as she closed the door, leaving all the fuss and noise outside.

Winnie and Anne came running from the bedroom so excited to see me that they barely noticed
the bike that was taking up half of the kitchen.

We all sat down and Mam gave a big sigh. 'Lily,
what have you done now?' she said.

'What do you mean?' I said innocently.

'Where on earth did you get that thing?' she asked.
'I know you can't afford a bicycle, or even a single one
of its wheels.'

'Oh,' I said. 'You see ...'

'I won't see anything if you don't hurry up and tell
me,' said Mam.

Once again I wished that I could tell Mam about
my friendship with Maeve. Once again, though, I
knew it was impossible. I hate lying to Mam, so I
told her a bit of the truth.

'Sir Josslyn bought the bicycle for Lady Mary,' I
said. 'But she didn't like it, so now I'm allowed to use
it every Saturday.'

'The Gore-Booths are decent people,' said Mam.

'But I hope you're not taking advantage of their good nature.'

'I'm not, I promise,' I said.

'Well, if you're sure,' said Mam. 'And I have to say, it's lovely to have you home a bit earlier, and you'll be able to stay later too.'

'Can I have a go on the bicycle?' asked Jimmy.

'Me first 'cause I'm older,' said Denis.

Mam shook her head. 'It's not a plaything, and Lily only has a loan of it. If I catch any of you even touching it, I'll take out the wooden spoon and ...'

The boys looked scared and I tried not to smile. Mam was always threatening the boys with the wooden spoon, but she never even took it down from the shelf unless she was baking bread.

'If you're good,' I said, trying to console the boys, 'I'll tell you all about Michael Gore-Booth and the baby seal.'

'Tell us about the seal!' said Anne, jumping up and down.

Winnie climbed up on my lap. 'Did you bring me a new dress?' she asked.

'No, silly. That was a special treat,' I said. 'But if we look in the basket we might just find something nice for you to eat.'

Everyone waited excitedly to see what treats Cook had sent, and to hear my stories, and Mam smiled at me. I loved being at home.

* * *

Even with all the extra time, the day went too quickly. When I wheeled the bicycle out of the house, there was a gathering of children on the road.

'What are you lot doing here?' asked Mam. 'Is there a procession or something on?'

They all laughed. 'We want to see Lily on the bike,' said Brendan.

'Oh, Lily,' said Mam, as she gave me my goodbye hug. 'You're the eighth wonder of the world!'

I didn't feel very wonderful as I sat on the saddle and pushed myself off. If I fell now, I'd be teased for the rest of my life. There was complete silence as I swayed and wobbled, but as I began to pedal, everyone cheered and clapped. All the children ran along beside me, whistling and shouting. I pedalled as fast as I could, and soon even Denis, the fastest runner in the village, was left behind.

'Bye, Lily,' he called.

'Bye, Denis,' I replied, and then I waved one hand in the air like a queen and went on my way.

* * *

Back at Lissadell, I put the bicycle back in the coach house, and used one of Albert's rags to wipe the splashes of mud off the black paint. When I got to our room, Nellie was sitting on her bed, waiting to hear the news of my day off.

'Going on the bicycle was the best thing,' I began.

'It was ...'

Before I could finish, there was a light knock on the door, and Nellie ran to open it.

'It's probably Isabelle ... Lady Mary!' she said. I could hear the shock in her voice.

Because of the way we lived, I spent many hours in Lady Mary's room, but she never, ever came to mine.

'Hello, Nellie,' said Lady Mary. 'I wonder if I could come in for a moment?'

And my heart sank right down to the toes of my shiny brown boots.

Chapter Nine

Lady Mary came into the room, which now felt very dull and shabby as I tried to see it through her eyes. I quickly bundled up my nightgown and shawl, which were thrown on the bed, and put them under my pillow. Nellie stood by the door as if she had turned to stone. She had a confused look on her face as if she had no idea why Lady Mary was there. Unfortunately, I was fairly sure I knew why, and the very thought of it made my hands shake as if I were chilled to the bone.

'May I sit?' asked Lady Mary, as if she didn't own the house and everything in it. As if she wasn't allowed to do exactly as she pleased.

I nodded, and as there was no chair, she sat on my bed.

'You two girls should sit down too,' she said, and

obediently Nellie and I sat side by side on Nellie's bed.

I felt sick to my stomach as we all looked at each other.

Should I have warned Nellie that I had asked Lady Mary to find out about her sisters?

Would that have made any difference at all?

'Nellie,' said Lady Mary gently. 'I understand that when you went to the workhouse, your two sisters went with you.'

Nellie nodded. She also gave a little shudder, but I couldn't tell if it was because of the mention of her sisters, or the workhouse.

'Your sister Lizzie was very unwell when she got there,' said Lady Mary. 'She had the same fever that took your poor mother and father.'

I wished this could be a fairytale with a happy ending for everyone, but Lady Mary's serious face told me my wish was not going to come true.

'I have made some enquiries,' she continued. 'And

I am afraid I have some very bad news for you. Nellie dear, poor little Lizzie was sent to the workhouse infirmary and she died a week later.'

I took Nellie's hand and squeezed it. 'Oh, Nellie,' I said. 'This is such sad news. I'm so sorry for you.'

Nellie was quiet. Why wasn't she screaming and crying the way I would have been if anything happened to Winnie or Anne?

Hadn't she understood Lady Mary's words?

Lady Mary came and sat beside Nellie and put her arm around her shoulder. 'Nellie, dear,' she said.

'It's all right,' said Nellie. 'Even before the fever, Lizzie was always chesty. Mam made her special drinks and I used to cry because I couldn't share them. I was little and I didn't understand, but I'm grown now, and I'm sorry I made such a fuss. For all these past years, I didn't dare to dream that Lizzie might be alive. Thank you for finding out about her, Lady Mary – and thank you for telling me.'

Nellie's eyes were dry, though I could barely see

them for the tears that were rolling down my cheeks.

'And your other sister, Johanna,' said Lady Mary. 'She was also very unwell.'

I brushed my tears away and waited.

Could Nellie have had all the bad luck in the world?

Was she going to hear that her whole family was dead?

But Lady Mary was smiling. 'For some reason, Johanna was sent to the workhouse in Tubercurry, and there, I'm very happy to say, she regained her health.'

Nellie still seemed numb, as if she could not understand either good news or bad – as if she were wrapped up in a thick fog that stopped her from feeling anything.

'And is she still there?' I asked. 'Is Johanna still in the workhouse in Tubercurry?'

Being in a workhouse was a terrible thing, but it had to be better than being dead.

'No,' said Lady Mary. 'Johanna is no longer there. If she had been, I would have ...'

She stopped, but I could guess what she was going to say. This lovely lady had gone to the workhouse in Tubercurry herself. If Johanna had been there, she would have rescued her, just as she had rescued Nellie.

'So where is she?'

Lady Mary sighed. 'The master of the workhouse was most unhelpful, and did not want to give me the information I needed, but I managed to persuade him in the end.'

Lady Mary is very sweet and gentle, but as she continued to speak, I realised that when she needed to, she could be as tough as iron. 'He told me that Johanna left the workhouse two years ago, and that she found employment as a maid.'

'Where?' I asked. 'Where is she working? Can Nellie go there? Can she see her sister at last?'

'Unfortunately it isn't as easy as that,' said Lady Mary. 'Eventually the master showed me her record,

and all it said was '*Discharged to domestic service, County Sligo*'.

'But Sligo is *huge*,' I said. 'She could be anywhere.'

But then I remembered that although Sligo is full of houses, most of them are small like Mam's little cottage. Very few families had room for servants, or money to pay them.

'I have already sent notes to all my friends in the county,' said Lady Mary. 'I have given them Johanna's name, and I have asked them to forward the details to their friends too. I am confident that before too long we will know where Johanna is. Be brave, Nellie. I am sure that soon, you and your sister will be reunited.'

As Lady Mary left the room, a young scullery maid came along the corridor. She was a new arrival at Lissadell, and very shy. When she saw Lady Mary coming out of our bedroom, she looked as if she had seen a ghost. I didn't feel like explaining everything to her, so I stuck out my tongue, and she ran away as

if I had hit her.

I closed the door, and went to sit next to my friend.

'All this has something to do with you, hasn't it, Lily?' she said. 'Did you ask Lady Mary to find out about my sisters?'

'Yes,' I said. 'I asked her to help. Nellie, I hope you're not sorry. Do you wish you didn't know about poor little Lizzie?'

She shook her head. 'No, I don't wish that. I never really, truly expected to see Lizzie again, so any secret hopes I had weren't real – and impossible hopes are no good at all. It's better that I know the truth.'

'You're very brave.'

'I don't have a choice, do I? Sitting here and crying won't make any difference.'

'But now we know that Johanna is out there some-where, and Lady Mary won't give up. She will find her, I know she will, and then ... oh, Nellie, are you very excited at the thought of seeing your sister again?'

As I said the words, I could see she wasn't excited at all. Her life had been so terrible, she had learned not to dream of better times.

'Let's wait and see what happens.'

I wouldn't sleep until we found Johanna, and couldn't understand how Nellie could bear to wait. Then I realised the truth – Nellie had spent most of her life waiting.

Chapter Ten

The next few weeks went by very slowly. I always tried to be in a corridor where I might see Lady Mary, and she must have wondered if I was following her around the house. It didn't matter anyway. Every time she saw me, she shook her head, and I knew she had no good news to share.

One day Lady Mary came over to me as I was dusting the breakfast room. I was glad to see her, as I was bored from lifting up the many precious vases and ornaments, and dusting underneath them. How could one family need so many things? In our house there was only one holy picture over the fireplace.

'Good morning, Lily,' said Lady Mary. 'I know you have been waiting for good news, but I am sorry to say that I have none. The last of my friends replied to me this morning, and she could not help. None of my

friends, or their friends, has seen or heard of Johanna Gallagher. I am beginning to think that even if she were once in service in Sligo, she isn't here any more.'

I had a sick feeling in my stomach.

Where could she be?

If Johanna was gone from Sligo, how would we ever find her?

Where would we even start to look?

What if she had gone all the way to Dublin – or London – or New York?

What if she had ... died?

Would Nellie ever know the truth?

And how would she go on if she did?

'I am sorry I couldn't bring you any good news,' said Lady Mary.

'I understand,' I said. 'Thank you for helping, Lady Mary. I am grateful to you, and so is Nellie.'

Lady Mary smiled at me, and I took my dusters and went back to Mrs Bailey to find out where I had to clean next.

The next day Maeve came back to stay, and I told her the story.

'Poor Nellie,' she said when I was finished. 'There has to be a way to find out where Johanna is.'

'Maybe there is a way,' I said. 'But I can't think of it.'

Suddenly she gave a huge smile. 'I know, what to do!' she said. 'Uncle Joss has a book called *Debrett's Peerage* – have you read it?'

'No. What's it about – and how will it help us to find Johanna?'

'It's a bit boring, actually, but grown-ups seem to like it. It's a big fat book with lists of people and their families, and their titles – it probably tells you where they live too – it might tell us where Johanna lives. Let's go and check right now. We can—'

She headed for the door, but stopped when she saw I wasn't following her.

'What is it, Lily? Do you want me to ask Mrs Bailey if …?'

'What kind of families are in that book?' I asked. 'Is your family in it?'

'Yes, we are – and so is my friend Stella, and, well, all of the people we know.'

'You mean people like you?'

Her face went red. 'Yes,' she said. 'I should have thought of that. It's all about people like me.'

I felt sorry for her. She was so protected, it was easy for her to forget how unequal the world was.

But then she smiled again. 'Maybe there's a book like that for servants. We could ask Mrs Bailey – she'd know, wouldn't she?'

'No one cares enough about servants to write a whole book about them. If we're lucky, we might get a job reference – and that's the only thing anyone will ever write down about us.'

'You must think I'm very foolish.'

'No,' I said. 'I think you're very kind, trying to find

a way to help Nellie.'

After that, I noticed that Maeve was extra-gentle whenever she saw Nellie. Nellie didn't react though. She was going around as if she were wearing a mask – a mask that made her look as if she were a walking, talking doll with no feelings at all. When I first arrived at Lissadell, Nellie had been grumpy and a little bit mean, but that was easier to cope with than the way she was now. I felt sorry for her – sorrier than I ever had for anyone, but sometimes I wanted to shake her, just to get a reaction, just so I could see that she was really alive.

* * *

Then one day Maeve came to me all flustered and excited.

'I have great news!' she said.

'Is it Johanna?' I asked. 'Has Lady Mary found her? Where is she? Is someone going to bring her here?'

'Oh no, Lily. I'm so sorry, the news is not about Johanna. It's about me.'

Maeve had so many things in her life. She travelled and went to garden parties and tennis afternoons and hunts and exhibitions. It was easy for her to forget about Nellie and her troubles. It wasn't so easy for me though. Except for my days off, every day was the same. I had little to distract me as I scrubbed and cleaned, spending hours and hours with Nellie, never being able to forget how sad her life was.

'What's your good news, Maeve?' I asked.

'Now I'm ashamed to even say.'

'Please say. I'd very much like to hear some good news.'

'Mother is coming to see me. She will be here tomorrow.'

'That *is* good news,' I said. Even though visitors meant more work for Nellie and me, at least they brightened up the place a little. And Countess Mark-ievicz, with her eccentric ways usually brightened up

the place a lot. 'When will she be here?'

'She arrives tomorrow evening, and leaves the next day.'

'That's a short visit.' I thought of all the work Nellie and I would have to do that evening, airing and dusting and preparing a room for Countess Markievicz – for one single day.

'I know. Mother is very busy in Dublin, but she has to come here because she wants to borrow money from Uncle Joss.'

'Will he give it to her?'

'He usually does – even though the two of them don't see eye to eye any more. He doesn't approve of her political views, and her life in Dublin. I don't know why he's so embarrassed by her – she's only fighting for a free and fair Ireland.'

I didn't know what to say to this. A free Ireland sounded like a good thing to me, but I'd heard men in my village saying that people like the Countess were only making trouble for everyone else.

'I think Mother would like to stay here longer,' she said. 'But I'm afraid if she did, she and Uncle Joss would end up having the most terrible row.'

'But only one single day!' Once again I felt sorry for Maeve. I saw my mother once a week, but months and months could pass without Maeve seeing hers.

Now Maeve gave a huge smile. 'She's only staying here at Lissadell for one day – but I will be leaving with her!'

'She's taking you to Dublin?'

I knew that living in Dublin with her mother was Maeve's dream, but where would that leave me? I would never see Maeve, and I would miss her so much. I could already imagine endless dreary days without her.

Maeve shook her head. 'No, Mother's not taking me to Dublin. We are going visiting for a few days.'

'Where?' I knew I'd never live a life where I'd be driving around Sligo, staying with friends who lived in big houses, and I couldn't help feeling a little jealous.

'Who cares? Temple House in Ballinacarrow I think.'

'That's miles away,' I said. 'My friend Hanora's aunt used to work near there and she only came home once a year.'

'It's not that far.' Then I realised that distances are different when you have a motor car to carry you around the country.

'We'll be visiting someone Mother was friends with when she was a little girl,' she said. 'I suppose they will talk about the past, and be terribly boring.'

I laughed. 'I can't imagine your mother being boring. Some of the stories you've told me make her sound very exciting.' I didn't mention that I'd heard other stories about Countess Markievicz from the footmen – ones that made my hair stand on end. They talked about her going on marches – and even being arrested!

'Lily! Lily where have you got to?'

It was Mrs Bailey and she sounded cross.

'I have to go,' I said. 'Enjoy your mother's visit, Maeve. I hope I will see her while she is here. It would be lovely.'

But then I stopped talking. I dearly wanted to see the Countess again, but Maeve and I both knew that unless I passed the Countess in a corridor, I was unlikely to see her at all. It wasn't as if I could sit down next to her and have a cup of tea and chat about her exciting life in Dublin.

Maeve smiled. 'I'll try to arrange something,' she said.

Before I could ask what she meant, Mrs Bailey called me again, and I ran off to do my endless work.

* * *

'Oh dear,' said Mrs Bailey later, as Nellie and I came back from cleaning the dressing rooms and laying out the towels. 'What are we to do? We are already up in a heap because of the Countesses visit, and

now this.'

'What is it?' I asked.

'Teresa has vanished. No one has seen her for hours, and all her things are gone from her room.'

I wasn't sad to hear that Teresa was gone. She was never nice to me, and she thought she was great, just because she was maid to Lady Mary. Recently she had met a young man, and I had heard rumours that they planned to run off together. Now it seemed they were more than rumours.

'It is a crisis,' said Mrs Bailey. 'Who will help Lady Mary to dress for dinner?'

I smiled. My little sister Anne has been able to dress herself for ages, and Winnie can do everything except put on her stockings. Why couldn't rich people do easy things like taking care of themselves, or cooking their dinner or lighting the fire?

'You will have to do it, Nellie,' said Mrs Bailey then. 'As housemaid, you're the person who should step up.'

Nellie's eyes opened wide in horror, as if Mrs Bailey had asked her to swim all the way to America.

'Not me,' she whispered. 'I wouldn't dare. I wouldn't know how.'

'Of course you can do it, Nellie,' I said, trying to encourage her. 'You dress yourself every morning don't you? You never have a problem with that.'

But poor Nellie didn't reply. Her face had gone pale, and her hands were shaking.

'Pull yourself together, child,' said Mrs Bailey, though I feared what she was asking was impossible. Nellie looked ready to faint away.

'I'll do it,' I said.

Mrs Bailey gave a big sigh. 'As under-housemaid it is not really appropriate, but in the circumstances, I suppose you will have to do. Now change into a fresh apron, and go at once to Lady Mary's room. Nellie, I hear the drawing room bell ringing – go and see what is needed.'

'Thank you, Lily,' whispered Nellie as she ran off.

'What are you waiting for, Lily?' asked Mrs Bailey.

Now I didn't feel so confident. I knew all about dusting and sweeping and lighting fires and things like that – I didn't know the first thing about being a lady's maid.

'What exactly am I supposed to ... do?' I asked.

'Oh dear, Lily,' said Mrs Bailey. 'You're such a competent girl, I sometimes forget how very young you are. Come in to the dining hall for a few minutes and I'll tell you what you need to know.

* * *

In the servants' dining hall, Mrs Bailey sat down, and I stood beside her with my hands clasped in front of me.

'I was a lady's maid once, you know – in my very first position in Galway. I took such pride in that work, I can tell you. My mistress was very, very pleased with

me, and when she moved to London, she gave me the most glowing reference. I could have obtained a job anywhere in the country.'

'I didn't know that,' I said politely, wondering if this conversation was going to be any help to me at all. Then Mrs Bailey remembered herself.

'Anyway,' she said. 'For tonight all you will have to do is help Lady Mary with her hair and her clothes. You can manage that can't you?'

'Yes, Mrs Bailey.'

'I haven't had time to talk to Lady Mary yet, but I expect you'll have to take over Teresa's everyday duties until we can find a replacement – and who knows how long that will take?'

Now I was very worried. 'What exactly are those duties?'

She took a deep breath. 'You bring Lady Mary her first cup of tea in the morning – ask Cook how she likes it. You are to take care of her clothes – check what needs repairing, and see to that – at least you

are capable with a needle, which is something. Then sort out her laundry, and remove any small stains. Wash the hairbrushes and combs, and lay them in the sun to dry. Tidy the jewellery, and check all the clasps and fasteners. Advise Lady Mary as she selects a suitable outfit, and lay it out in the dressing room for her. Do the same thing for her mid-day outfits and in the evening. If she is going away for a night, you have to pack everything she needs. After dinner, you are usually free, but you may not go to bed until Lady Mary does. You have to be available if she needs anything at all.'

I was starting to feel sorry I'd volunteered for the job.

Just then the clock chimed, and Mrs Bailey jumped to her feet.

'Look at the time,' she said. 'Lady Mary will be waiting, so run along quickly.'

'Yes, Mrs Bailey. Thank you for telling me all I need to know.'

'My dear girl, that is not one tenth of what you need to know, but it will have to do for now.'

Chapter Eleven

'I have already done my hair and laid out my clothes,' said Lady Mary.

I turned away so she wouldn't see me smile. She was acting as if laying out her own clothes was a very big thing. But then, maybe with so many clothes to choose from, it *was* a big thing. I only owned two dresses and my uniform, and one pair of boots, so I didn't have to make big decisions five times a day.

There wasn't very much for me to do. Lady Mary managed to put on her dress all on her own, and turned so I could do up the tiny pearl buttons on the back. Then I handed her her beautiful cream silk shoes, and tied the button at the ankle.

'Pass me my perfume, please, Lily,' she said.

Her dressing table was full of bottles and jars, and I had no idea which one was perfume. I picked the one

I thought looked prettiest, a tall glass bottle with foreign writing on the side. I knew I was right when she took the bottle and dabbed perfume onto her wrists, filling the room with the scent of violets.

'Oh, Lady Mary,' I said. 'It's like being outside in a field of—' I put my hand over my mouth, remembering I wasn't supposed to talk to her unless she talked to me first.

She smiled at me. 'It's very beautiful, isn't it? It was a present from the Countess – it came all the way from Czechoslovakia.'

As she handed me the bottle, I was terrified I'd drop it, and my hand shook as I put it carefully back where I'd found it.

'Which necklace do you think?' she asked, opening one of her many jewellery boxes. 'The pearls? Or the sapphire? Or maybe the gold locket Sir Josslyn bought me when Michael was born?'

She held up the locket, and I watched as it swung from its delicate gold chain. I could see the tiny hinge

for opening it, and though I dearly wanted to know what was inside, I didn't dare to ask.

'Would you like to see inside?' she asked, as if she could read my mind.

Before I could answer, she opened the locket and I leaned closer to see.

'It's a tiny lock of hair from each of the babies,' she said. 'All tied together with a silk thread. It is very special to me.'

I sighed. What my mam would give to be a fine lady, with a real gold locket and a special place to keep a few hairs from each of her babies' heads. She would wear it every single moment, and never wish for another necklace in all her days.

'The locket is beautiful, Lady Mary,' I said. 'I think you should wear it.'

'Then I will,' she said, and she turned so I could fasten it behind her neck.

I couldn't help feeling very important as I helped her to choose between a grey satin wrap and a soft

blue wool one. Then she sat at her dressing table and I stood with my hands clasped together, and wondered what I was supposed to do next.

Lady Mary took out a number of rings, and held them in her hand, deciding which to wear. Being rich seemed to involve a lot of decisions that never bothered the likes of me.

'How is Nellie doing?' she asked, as she put on a gold ring with a huge ruby-red stone.

'I think she is sad – but with Nellie, it isn't easy to tell.'

'Poor girl. If there is anything I can do, please let me know.'

'You have given her a good job, and a warm bed to sleep in every night. After that I don't think there's anything ... oh, Lady Mary, I wish I could do something to help her.'

'You are a good friend to Nellie,' she said, smiling. 'That must be a big comfort to her – and sometimes that is all you can do. Just listen to her, and be kind.'

Lady Mary was so gentle and wise, and I knew she was right. Still, I wasn't happy. Doing nothing made me feel so helpless.

'Well then,' she said, standing up and straightening her dress. 'I think I am ready. Thank you for your help, Lily.'

She picked up her beaded silk evening bag, and as she did, a few small coins fell to the floor. I knelt and picked up the coins, and handed them to her, feeling embarrassed as my coarse, work-worn hands touched Lady Mary's soft, white skin.

'Oh dear,' she said. 'My favourite bag is ripped. It used to belong to my mother, and I love it so.'

'May I see?'

I took the bag from her and examined where the silk had worn away on one side.

'I think I might be able to mend this,' I said.

'If you're sure?'

I didn't want to make any promises, so I nodded my head and stood there awkwardly, not knowing if

I should stay or go.

'You may leave, Lily,' she said. 'Thank you.'

'And what about tomorrow? Mrs Bailey told me the things a lady's maid is supposed to do – and I think I could manage them all.'

She smiled. 'I'm sure you could manage very well, but for now I think it best if you only help me to dress in the evenings. The rest of the time Mrs Bailey will need you to do your usual work with Nellie.'

I was disappointed. I had liked the idea of helping with Lady Mary's clothes and jewellery. I liked the idea of spending more time with this kind, elegant woman. But at Lissadell, no one ever asked me what I wanted to do, so I thanked her politely and went back to my real life.

* * *

The next morning, I heard all the fuss as Countess Markievicz arrived with her little dog, Poppet. I

couldn't see them though, as I was on my knees helping Nellie to polish the night nursery floors.

'I wish I could see her,' I sighed, using my arm to wipe a stray strand of hair from my eyes. 'It's not fair that rich people have all the fun while we have to stay here working all the time.'

'When you're a teacher you'll still have to work,' said Nellie.

I loved that she said 'when' and not 'if'.

'I know,' I said. 'But that will be different. I will be teaching little children, helping them with their sums and reading.'

'But you'll still have to light the classroom fire, and clean the windows, and scrub the floors when the children go home.'

'But don't you see, Nellie? That will be so different. I will be doing work I want to do. I will be living the life I have always dreamed of.'

'I love working at Lissadell,' said Nellie.

'I know you do, and that's lucky, because neither

of us has a choice in the matter. Times are changing though, Nellie. I listen to the footmen reading the newspapers, and I know what's going on in the world. Soon people like us will have a choice.'

'What do you mean?'

'I mean, if you want to work at Lissadell, you can, but you will be able to decide that for yourself. Soon people like us will have opportunities our parents could only dream of.'

'My parents only dreamed of feeding us, and staying alive – and they weren't even able to do that.'

'Oh, Nellie. I'm so sorry for them, and for you. But that's why things like that won't happen in the future. That's why ...'

Just then Mrs Bailey appeared. 'Move along, girls,' she said. 'You're needed in the china room, so finish that and follow me.'

I rolled my eyes behind her back. 'Opportunities,' I whispered to Nellie, and she laughed.

* * *

After I had polished about a thousand fine china cups, I had to fight to stop myself throwing one at the wall. Who could ever need all these cups – and why did they have to be so shiny?

I heard a bell ringing, and looked at the board on the wall in the corridor.

'It's the large drawing room,' I said. 'Don't worry, Nellie, I'll go.'

She smiled. We both knew why I wanted to go upstairs.

* * *

Sir Josslyn was standing looking out the window, and the Countess was seated in an armchair in the corner of the room. She looked like a queen, tall and elegant and dressed in dark green silk. Maeve was sitting on a stool by her feet, and Lady Mary was in

her usual chair by the fire. Lady Mary was so sweet and gentle, and I wondered if she might be afraid of the Countess, who was like a swirling firestorm.

'Hello, Lily,' said Lady Mary.

The Countess smiled when she heard my name. 'Ah, Lily,' she said.

I blushed. Did she actually remember me from the time she helped me to carry a huge bucket of coal up the back staircase?

Was I more than just another servant to her?

But then she continued. 'You're the girl Maeve has been telling me about.'

Now I blushed even more.

Was she angry because Maeve and I had become friends?

Was she going to ask Lady Mary to fire me?

But if so, why was she smiling?

'Maeve tells me she has been painting your portrait,' she continued. 'And I'm very happy to hear it.'

Would she be happy if she heard that Maeve had

long ago given up the notion of painting me? What if she actually wanted to see a painting, and Maeve had nothing to show her? I looked desperately at Maeve, but she was petting Poppet and didn't seem worried. Maybe it was easier for her. If anyone was going to get into trouble, I knew it would be me.

'Yes, Lady, I mean Countess, I mean Madame.' I was all red and flustered, and ready to apologise, though it wasn't even my fault.

Then Lady Mary saved me. 'We rang the bell because there's been a bit of a spill, Lily,' she said. 'Could you please bring a bucket and a brush and clean it up for us?'

I had been so busy looking at Countess Markievicz, I hadn't noticed that the tea tray had fallen from the side table, and the rug was covered in a mess of broken china, and tea and milk and cakes and sweets.

'I did it,' said Maeve. 'Silly me.'

I looked at her and she winked, and all at once I understood what had happened. She had told me

she'd find a way for me to see her mother, and had deliberately knocked over the tray so either Nellie or I would be called to clean it. I didn't dare to wink back at her as I hurried from the room to get what I needed.

When I got back to the drawing room, Maeve and Lady Mary were talking quietly, while Countess Markievicz and Sir Josslyn were arguing. No one paid any attention to me, as I very slowly picked the broken china from the rug, and did my best to clean up the mess.

'When are you going to stop drawing attention to yourself, Constance?' asked Sir Josslyn. 'Our mother is ashamed, and our poor father would turn in his grave if he knew half of what is said about you in the newspapers.'

'Our parents always encouraged us to think of others,' said the Countess. 'I should think they would be proud of me, feeding the starving children and helping people less fortunate than myself.'

'Perhaps you could help them in a less conspicuous way?'

The Countess snorted. She didn't look as if she knew how to be inconspicuous.

'And is it true that you have been wearing ... breeches ... in public?' he said.

Now she laughed. 'Oh, Joss, you are so old-fashioned. Of course I have been wearing breeches. One day that will be commonplace for women.'

'Never!' said Sir Josslyn, looking as if she had suggested that one day women would be able to fly.

'How are we supposed to fight if we are wearing skirts?' she asked, and then smiled as her brother looked ill at the thought.

'Enough, Constance,' he said weakly. 'Enough.'

'Did I ever tell you that the poor women of Dublin gave me an illuminated scroll, to thank me for feeding them during the Lockout?' she said.

'That's very nice for you,' he said. 'But the Lockout is over now, so maybe you could settle down a bit –

write some poetry or take up hunting again?'

'I'll settle down when Ireland is free,' she said. 'And not a moment before.'

I had finished tidying up, but I was so interested in the argument, I stayed kneeling on the rug with my mouth open.

'Lily,' said Lady Mary quietly. 'If you are finished you may leave us.'

I scrambled to my feet, afraid she was cross, but as I hurried from the room I could see that she was trying to hide her smile.

Chapter Twelve

For the next few days, while Mrs Bailey was trying to find someone to take Teresa's place, I helped Lady Mary to dress in the evenings. I looked forward to the time I spent in her room, admiring her nice things, and helping her with small jobs. She talked a lot about her children, saying how happy Michael was now that he had Spotty the seal to take care of, how Hugh wanted a pony, how Bridget loved listening to stories, and how baby Brian had a new tooth. I tried not to feel jealous as I thought how much her children had, compared to my own dear brothers and sisters.

* * *

'Did you notice that Maggie and Delia barely spoke

to me at dinner today?' I said, as Nellie and I were getting ready for bed one evening. 'And some of the others were quite rude too. Even Harry wasn't as friendly as he usually is.'

'Er, not really – I didn't notice that.' Nellie was too honest to be a good liar.

I looked into her bright blue eyes. 'There's something you're not telling me, isn't there?'

She went red. 'It's ... you see, oh, I'm sorry, Lily ... didn't you know – no one ever likes or trusts a lady's maid?'

'I know no one liked Teresa – but that's because she was horrible – but I'm not like that – and I'm not even a proper lady's maid.'

'It's not about Teresa. I've heard the others talking, and they say that's the way it always is in big houses. Servants are afraid that the lady's maid spends too much time with the lady of the house. She's a little bit in their world, and a little bit in ours.'

'And why does that matter?'

'*I* know you won't change, but the others don't. They're afraid you might get too friendly with Lady Mary – that you might tell tales on them – that you might be sort of ... a spy.'

I didn't know whether to laugh or cry. Why did there have to be so many rules? People were only people, so why did some have to act one way, and some act another way? It didn't seem fair.

But none of that was Nellie's fault. 'Thank you for telling me the truth,' I said.

And the next day, when I walked into the dining hall and everyone stopped talking, I stood on a chair and said in my loudest voice, 'I'm one of you, and I always will be. I'll never be a spy, and if anyone says different I'll ... I'll ... I'll set Spotty the seal on you!'

For a second there was silence, and then everyone started to laugh. Harry patted my shoulder as I went to my place, and a new young footman made seal noises.

'That's enough drama out of you, Lily,' said Mrs

Bailey as I sat down, but I could see she was trying not to smile.

And after that everything was fine.

* * *

In my room, late at night, while Nellie was practising her reading, I worked on Lady Mary's evening bag. It was a difficult job, but I wanted to do it right. I very much wanted to impress her.

On the fourth day I brought the bag to Lady Mary. She took it from me and examined it closely, turning it over and over. Then she unfastened it and looked inside. Her silence was making me nervous.

'Is there something wrong, Lady Mary?' I asked. 'Don't you like it? I did my very best work.'

She put the bag on her dressing table and smiled at me. 'It is simply perfect,' she said. 'It is as good as new – the mend is invisible. There were some beads missing on the front, and I see you have replaced them. I

am mystified, though. Where did you find beads to match so well?'

I could feel my face going pink. I was pleased with what I had done, but hoped she wouldn't be cross with me. 'I ... I made the strap a little shorter, and used the beads from the cut-off piece. I hope you don't mind. I couldn't think of any other way to make it nice again.'

'How inventive of you!' she said. 'You are a little genius.'

I had a smile on my face for the rest of the evening.

* * *

A few days later, Mrs Bailey asked me to dust the golden birds on the main staircase. I loved that job, as it was nice and easy, and gave me a good view of the hallway, so I could see who was coming and going.

As I got to the bottom of the stairs, Maeve's grand-mother, Lady Georgina, came through the front door,

where she met Sir Josslyn who was on his way out.

'Mother,' he said, kissing her on the cheek. 'I didn't expect to see you so early. Is Maeve with you? I am going to check on my new anemones and she might like to come along and help me.'

'I have left that naughty girl at Ardeevin,' she said. 'Since her mother left she has been quite difficult.'

I stood there pretending to concentrate on my work. Poor Maeve. No wonder she was 'difficult'. Her mother had gone away, and who knew when they would see each other again?

'She threw a big tantrum when I said she couldn't come. She said she had something very important to do when she got here – just a story, I suppose.' But then Lady Georgina spoke in a softer voice. 'I know she is sad,' she said. 'I have left her with Miss Clayton to do some extra lessons to make up for the time she was away. I will send for her tomorrow, and I am sure she will be happy to help with your project then.'

Sir Josslyn went out and after handing her coat to

the footman, Lady Georgina came towards the stairs. I held my duster behind my back, and stood out of the way, with my head down. When she stopped right next to me I couldn't help feeling nervous. I knew she was a good, kind woman, but still I was terrified of her. I examined her pretty grey shoes, with fancy buttons all along the sides, hoping she had only stopped to catch her breath.

'You are Lily, aren't you?' she asked.

I looked up at her. 'Yes, Lady Georgina. Can I do something for you?'

'I have been talking to Lady Mary about you.'

I knew I hadn't done anything wrong, but I still felt guilty. Why would they be talking about *me*?

'She showed me the evening bag that you mended, and I have to say that it is the finest work I have ever seen. You are a clever girl.'

'Thank you, Lady Georgina.'

'I take it you know about the needlework school I set up?'

Lady Mary had told me about the school. Lady Georgina had set it up many years earlier, so that the poor women on the estate could learn a skill, and earn some extra money. Nellie said that during hard times the school saved many women from starving.

'Yes, Lady Georgina,' I said.

'And have you seen the needlework school?'

I smiled to myself. Did she think servants like me got an official tour of the estate?

'No, Lady Georgina. I haven't seen it.'

'That is a pity. I have to say I am very proud of the school. It has been running since the 1860s, you know. The instructors are quite skilled, and the women are turning out some very nice garments.'

She stood there for a minute, and I didn't know if I should go back to my work, or wait for her to say something else.

'Harry,' she called suddenly, and the footman came over. 'Please give me back my coat. Lily and I are going for a little walk.'

Harry returned her coat, and held it for her to put on. Then she took the duster from my hand and gave it to him.

'Tell Mrs Bailey that Lily will be back in twenty minutes.'

I wasn't sure where she was taking me, but I liked the idea of a little adventure, so I smiled at Harry, and he winked back at me. I followed Lady Georgina out the front door, down the steps and through the *porte cochere*. Soon it became clear that we were going towards the coach house, and I wondered if we were possibly going out in the motor car. I wondered if that would be excellent or terrifying.

But instead of going to where the car was kept, Lady Georgina led me through the coach house courtyard to a different building. She smiled at me as she opened the door and started up the flight of stairs. 'This is the needlework school,' she said, 'I thought you might like to see it.'

* * *

It was like heaven. It was a cosy room, with lots of light coming in through the many windows. It was a chilly day, but the stove in the centre of the room gave out lovely heat. Women from the estate were sitting at tables, and many of them were singing as they worked at their sewing and crochet. Everyone looked up and greeted Lady Georgina, but no one paid any attention to me.

'That's the instructor, Miss Connor,' said Lady Georgina, pointing at a serious-looking woman who was sitting at a desk, writing in a large book. 'And there's the assistant, Miss Flanagan.' Now she nodded towards a younger woman who was walking around the room, helping any women who asked for assistance.

'Some of the workers are very skilled when they arrive, but some women need a lot of help, and it does my heart good to see how they go on to do such

beautiful work. Come,' she said, leading me to a large table at the corner of the room. 'Here are some of the garments that are ready for sale.'

I gasped as I looked at the precious things. There was a perfect embroidered christening gown, some crocheted baby jackets, a few children's dresses, and underclothes fit for a queen. I wanted to touch everything, but didn't dare.

'They are so beautiful,' I said. 'Who buys them? Who can afford such lovely things? Do people come here to do their shopping? Are these things very expensive?'

I was so excited that I had forgotten I was only supposed to speak to the family if they spoke to me first.

Lady Georgina smiled at me, as if she hadn't noticed my mistake. 'The prices are reasonable, I hope,' she said. Then she picked up a small book. 'This is the catalogue. Buyers order from this, and we send them what they want.'

I took the book and turned the pages slowly. There was a description of each garment, a price, and then a drawing. The prices may well have been reasonable, but I knew if my poor mam had that much money, it would be spent on food for the table or turf for the fire. She would never even dream of owning such precious things.

Lady Georgina seemed to be waiting for me to say something.

'The drawings are beautiful,' I said.

'Thank you. I did those myself.'

Now I knew why her daughter Constance, and grand-daughter Maeve were so good at art. This was a very artistic family. But then maybe my family would be the same – if we didn't have to work so hard, and had time to practise drawing and painting. For my family, simply living took up most of our time.

I followed Lady Georgina as she walked around the room chatting to the women. She knew them all by name, and they seemed to like her.

I'm not sure how much time had passed, but I didn't want to leave. I didn't want to go back to the hurry and bustle of the main house. I wanted to stay in this warm, calm place forever.

Chapter Thirteen

It was late in the evening, and my work was all done. I was walking towards my bedroom, looking forward to spending some quiet time with Nellie. Isabelle had lent us a bundle of new books from the nursery, and I wanted to help Nellie to read some of the harder ones.

'Lily, Lily, I have something to tell you.'

Maeve came rushing towards me, taking me by surprise. I hadn't even known she was back.

'What do you have to tell me, Maeve?' I asked. 'Is it about your mother? I know you must miss her now that she has gone back to Dublin.'

'No. I mean yes. I do miss Mother, but that's not what I want to tell you. I have some very good news, and I have been dying to tell you for days, but Gaga wouldn't let me come here until tonight. I've been so

impatient, and I begged and begged but she wouldn't listen to me and ...'

'Are you going to tell me or not?' Of course I was happy that my friend had good news, but I was tired, and I guessed that the news was going to be about her, and not about Nellie or me.

'You know I was in Temple House with Mother this week?'

'Yes,' I said. 'And you thought it was going to be boring, but maybe it wasn't since you are so excited to tell me about it.'

'Well, it's just a very big, very boring house and I thought I'd never get out of there. Mother and Mrs Perceval talked and talked about things that did not interest me in the slightest, but on the last morning, something wonderful happened.'

'What?'

'I saw Mrs Perceval's lady's maid.'

'You did?' Maeve and I came from very different worlds, and often misunderstood each other. I had no

idea why she was excited about seeing a maid. Lissadell House was full of maids, and except for Nellie and me, Maeve didn't pay them very much attention.

'Yes – and this maid had very white skin and curly red hair, and bright blue eyes and ...'

At last I was beginning to understand. 'Oh, Maeve, do you think ...?'

'Except that her nose is rounder than Nellie's, they are exactly alike. Lily, I think I have found Nellie's sister.'

I jumped up and down. 'That's so ...' Then I stopped jumping. This was real life, not one of the fairy-tales in the nursery books. 'But Lady Mary wrote to all the big houses – and no one had ever heard of Nellie's sister. It has to be a mistake.'

'Maybe Aunt Mary forgot to write to Temple House? Or maybe they were away when the letter arrived? Or maybe Nellie's sister used to work somewhere else and only went to work there this week?'

I still wasn't sure. 'Did you talk to this girl? Did you

ask her if she came from the workhouse? Did you ask if she had a little sister called Nellie?'

'I didn't have time to talk to her. Mother and I were leaving, and Mother had a train to catch and the car was waiting for us. I know I'm right, though. Trust me, Lily, it's not a mistake. This girl was Nellie's double. They have to be sisters.'

And so she convinced me. 'Come on,' I said, hurrying along the corridor. 'Let's tell Nellie the great news.'

* * *

Nellie smiled when I came into the room. 'At last you're here, Lily,' she said. 'I can't work out what this word is ... M.A.G.I.C.A.L.'

'Magical,' I said without thinking. Then Maeve followed me into the room. Nellie dropped the book, looking guilty, even though she knew the children's nurse was happy for her to borrow it. She pulled

her blanket up to her chin, and I could tell she was ashamed of her old, patched nightgown.

'Nellie,' said Maeve. 'I have some wonderful news.'

'What is it?' And even though Nellie always tried hard not to hope for or dream of anything, I saw a light come into her eyes as she whispered the words.

'I've found your sister,' said Maeve.

Nellie's face went even paler than usual, making the freckles on her nose stand out like spatters of gold paint on a snow-white page.

'Are you sure? You've found her? You've really found Johanna?'

And as Maeve's smile faded, I knew there had been a terrible mistake. I wanted to kick myself. Why had I let Maeve tell Nellie about the girl, without even checking what she was called? What kind of a friend was I to let this happen?

'Her name wasn't Johanna,' whispered Maeve. 'I'm so sorry, Nellie, the girl I saw was called Susan.'

I could feel tears come to my eyes, but Nellie's eyes

were dry. For a moment it seemed that I was more disappointed than she was.

'My sister's name is Johanna,' she said quietly. 'She was called after my dad's mam. Lizzie was called after my mam's mam, and Mam picked my name because she thought it was beautiful.'

Then she picked up her book and began to turn the pages. Maeve looked at me uncertainly, and I felt sorry for her too. Just like me, she had wanted to help, and it wasn't her fault that between the two of us we had made a terrible mistake.

'I'm sorry, Nellie,' she said.

'Lots of girls have red hair,' said Nellie, without looking up. 'It was an easy mistake to make.'

'Maybe you should go back upstairs, Maeve,' I said. 'I'll take care of Nellie.'

'I can take care of myself,' said Nellie in a small voice. 'I always have.'

'I'm sorry, Nellie,' said Maeve again as she opened the door. 'That girl Susan was so like you, I was sure

she had to be your sister. I won't give up, I promise. I'll keep on looking until we find Johanna.'

Nellie didn't answer, and she was probably thinking the same as me. The world is a very big place, and how do you find one young girl in all the crowds?

* * *

That night I barely slept. Across the room, Nellie was tossing and turning, and though I whispered her name many times, she never answered.

I awoke to hear Delia, one of the kitchen maids, banging on the door.

'Lily, Nellie. It's late. Wake up.'

'Coming,' I said, and I heard the sound of Delia's heavy boots going back towards the kitchen.

Nellie and I jumped out of bed at the same time, stretching and rubbing our eyes.

Nellie looked so pale and lost. I wanted to hug her, but there was no time, and I feared she would push

me away.

'I'm sorry about yesterday,' I said. 'You shouldn't blame Maeve. It was mostly my fault, and I wish it hadn't happened.'

'It's all right,' said Nellie, pulling her uniform over her head. 'It's over now, and I don't want to talk about it any more.'

I wanted to use Mam's saying about sharing troubles, but Nellie didn't look as if she wanted to hear any of Mam's wise words, and right then I felt guilty for even having a mam.

'If that's what you want,' I said, and I pulled on my own uniform, ready for another long day of work.

* * *

Nellie went straight to the storeroom where the cleaning things were kept, but I ran to the kitchen. We weren't supposed to have breakfast until the downstairs rooms had been cleaned, but Cook knew

how hungry I was in the mornings, so she always gave me something small to eat before I did anything else.

'Lily,' she said, handing me a piece of bread and butter. 'You're so late – I thought you were never coming.'

'Thank you, Cook,' I said. 'You have just saved my life.'

She laughed. 'That's what you say every morning.'

As I turned to go, Maggie, the laundry maid came into the kitchen with a bundle of towels.

'Good morning, Lily,' she said.

I stared at her as if I had seen a ghost.

'Lily, are you all right?' she asked.

Cook came over and put her hand on my forehead. 'Lily, pet,' she said. 'What is it. You're as white as the freshly laundered sheets.'

'I'm fine,' I said. 'Really I'm fine.'

I turned and gave Maggie a big hug. 'Thank you so much,' I said.

She stared at me. 'But I didn't ...'

'I have to go,' I said. 'If Mrs Bailey is looking for me, tell her ... well I don't care what you tell her. I'll be back in a minute.'

Then I ran from the room, leaving Cook and Maggie staring after me as if I had lost my mind.

Chapter Fourteen

I ran up two flights of the servants' staircase, and carefully opened the door onto the corridor where the family had their bedrooms. I peeped out, but luckily no one was around. I wasn't supposed to be there until the family was down at breakfast, and I knew I'd be in trouble if anyone saw me. I always seemed to be breaking rules at Lissadell, but right then I didn't care.

I tiptoed along the corridor to Maeve's bedroom and tapped on the door.

I heard a sleepy voice. 'Whoever it is, go away. It's still dark.'

For a second I felt a touch of jealousy. Lucky Maeve never had to get up until it was light outside. Did she have any idea how much work I had done before she opened her eyes each morning? But then

I remembered why I was there and I pushed my jealousy aside.

I tiptoed into the room, closing the door softly behind me.

'I said go away. It's the middle of the night.'

'It's me, Lily,' I said, feeling my way towards the bed.

'What is it? Is something wrong? Is it Nellie? Wait a minute while I turn on the light.'

Just as my eyes were getting used to the darkness, Maeve sat up and lit the gas light, making the room cosy. She pulled a soft woollen shawl over her beautiful cotton nightgown.

'Here,' she said, patting the bed beside her. 'Sit down and tell me what's wrong.'

'Nothing's wrong,' I said. 'Something is very right.'

'Don't talk in riddles. I'm still only half awake.'

'How sure are you that the girl you saw at Temple House was Nellie's sister?'

'I told you yesterday. I was very, very sure, but now

we know it can't be her.'

'But maybe it *was* her after all.'

'I don't understand.'

'I was in the kitchen a few minutes ago and I saw Maggie, and ...' Now I was so excited I could barely get the words out.

'Maggie? Isn't she the laundry maid?'

'Yes, but her name isn't really Maggie.'

'Now I really don't understand. What has Maggie got to do with this?'

I took a deep breath. 'When I came here first, I met Maggie and told her that I liked her name, and she said that it wasn't her real name. Her real name is Agnes, but because there was already a kitchen maid here with that name, Mrs Bailey said she had to change it.'

'That's not very fair. I like being called Maeve and I wouldn't change my name for anyone.'

'You're rich – it won't ever happen to you.'

'Sorry,' she said, as if she needed to apologise for

being who she was.

'Anyway, don't you see? If Maggie ... or Agnes had to change her name, then ...'

Now Maeve gave a big smile. 'Then Susan could easily be Johanna.'

'Easily. Probably. Didn't you say that Temple House is very big?'

'It's huge. They have so many servants you wouldn't believe it. So they could easily have had a Johanna, and then made Nellie's sister change her name.'

'And it was probably the housekeeper who did that, so when Lady Mary asked if there was a Johanna Gallagher at Temple House, Mrs Perceval didn't know who that was.'

'This is so wonderful,' said Maeve. 'Have you told Nellie yet?'

'No, I came straight here. Nellie is probably still in the maids' storeroom, waiting for me to share my bread and butter with her, the way I usually do.'

As I said the words, I realized I was still holding

the piece of bread that Cook had given me. I broke it carefully and gave half to Maeve.

'Anyway,' I said as we ate. 'Until we're sure, I don't think we should say a word to Nellie. If we're wrong again ...'

'Agreed. For now this has to be our secret.'

'So how are we going to find out the truth?'

Maeve jumped out of bed. 'It's simple. I will go to Temple House and talk to Susan or Johanna, or whatever her name is.'

'How will you get there?'

'I'll go on the bicycle.'

Maeve was very serious, and I loved how far she was prepared to go to help Nellie, but I had to laugh.

'Oh how I'd love to see you cycling all those miles like a wild woman, but it's much too far. It would take you a day and a night – maybe even more.'

'You're right. I suppose I'll have to ask Albert to bring me. Let's hope he's not driving Uncle Joss today.'

'No,' I said. 'This isn't something you can do on your own. Why don't you ask Lady Mary to help? She's very kind, and we know how sorry she is for Nellie, so maybe ...'

'You're right. I'll ask Aunt Mary as soon as she gets up, and I'll let you know.'

I was relieved for a second, and then I remembered who I was and where I was.

'I have to go,' I said, running from the room.

In the drawing room, Nellie was crossly cleaning the first of the fireplaces. I was sorry I'd given away her bread, but told myself she wouldn't care, if she knew why.

* * *

Nellie and I were enjoying our breakfast in the kitchen when Maeve appeared, all dressed up in her coat and hat. Nellie stopped eating, and Cook jumped up from her stool and stood stiffly next to the chopping table,

but Maeve didn't notice. She never noticed how the servants jumped to attention when she appeared.

'Lily,' she said. 'Can I have a word with you please?'

I followed her into the corridor. 'It's all arranged,' she said. 'Albert is going to bring Aunt Mary and me to Temple House.'

'When?'

'In a few minutes. Mrs Perceval is going on a trip tonight, so Aunt Mary wants to get there before she leaves.'

'Will Lady Mary be cross if I'm wrong about Johanna?'

'No. She'll be disappointed, like all of us. But I don't think you're wrong.'

Now I started to see more problems.

'And if I'm right, if it's really Johanna, what will happen then? How will we get Nellie and her sister together?'

'I've been thinking about that,' she said. 'I'm hoping that when Johanna – if it's her – has a day off, Mrs

Bailey would give Nellie a day off too. I think Aunt Mary would let Albert to bring her to Temple House, and they could spend a few hours together. What do you think?'

I smiled. 'I think that if we could arrange that, Nellie will be the happiest girl in all of Sligo.'

* * *

'What did Maeve want?' asked Nellie when I went back to my breakfast. 'Is she going to paint you again? Or are the two of you going out on the bicycle?'

'Oh, Maeve isn't going to paint me. She only … she told me that she's going for a drive with Lady Mary.'

'Why did she bother telling you that?' asked Nellie, scraping the last of the porridge from her bowl.

'Who knows? Now pass the sugar. I'm starving.'

Chapter Fifteen

I spent the whole day looking out the windows, waiting for the motor car to come back. In the end, Nellie noticed how agitated I was.

'What is it, Lily,' she asked. 'Why do you keep looking out the window?'

I desperately wanted to tell her the truth, but I knew that was impossible. What if Maeve and I were wrong? Nellie was trying hard to be tough and brave and all grown up, but I knew that somewhere, deep inside, was a terrified and lonely little girl.

'Oh, it's such a nice day,' I said. 'I wish I were outside, that's all.'

She looked at me doubtfully, and then we returned to our work.

I knew Maeve and Lady Mary wouldn't be back for lunch, but my heart sank when I heard Cook

complaining that they weren't going to be there for dinner either.

Where could they be?

Had something gone wrong?

Why were they taking so long?

* * *

'I'm so tired,' said Nellie, putting her hand over her mouth, but not managing to hide her huge yawn.

Sir Josslyn and Lady Georgina had gone to bed, and Nellie and I were giving the front hall a final sweep and dust.

'At least this is the last job of the day,' I said. 'And we'll be in bed before you know it.'

'I can't wait,' she said, yawning again. 'And I won't read a word of my book tonight. I think I'll be asleep before my head hits the pillow.'

I ran my duster over the ugly stuffed secretary bird that was displayed on a shelf.

'I'm scared of that thing,' said Nellie.

'Me too, but I'm afraid that if I don't dust it every day it might come back to life and fly into my nightmares. It's so—'

And then, finally, I heard the sound of an engine and the crunch of wheels on the gravel.

'Oh,' said Nellie without much interest. 'Sounds like Lady Mary and Maeve are back.'

I began to panic, and I knew I needed time to think.

Would Nellie be cross that I hadn't told her why Lady Mary and Maeve had gone all the way to Temple House?

What if the news wasn't good?

'You know, I'm not so tired, Nellie,' I said. 'And I can see that you're exhausted. Why don't you go on to bed, and I'll finish up here?'

Nellie was usually very fair about work, and always made sure to do her share, if not more. Luckily though, she was so tired, she actually agreed without arguing.

'All right,' she said. 'Thank you. I'll just finish off this bit of sweeping and—'

The motor car had driven into the *porte cochere* and I could hear the creak as one of the doors opened.

'No!' I said quickly. 'Just go. If Lady Mary needs some jobs done you could be up for another hour. Leave your brush, leave everything, and go to bed.'

'Thank you, Lily,' she said as she hurried off towards the back stairs. 'You're such a good friend to me.'

I picked up her sweeping brush and stood like a statue, wondering if what she said was true.

* * *

Time seemed to stand still, which didn't make any sense as I could hear the large clock behind me ticking the seconds by. I could hear the opening and closing of car doors, and then the sound of the motor car driving away towards the coach house. Harry, the footman appeared and stood ready to take coats.

Then, after what felt like a lifetime, the huge front door opened.

Lady Mary came in first, smiling as she handed her coat to Harry. Then Maeve came in. She looked tired, but she had a huge smile on her face. And then ...

'Nellie?' I whispered, as a girl walked into the hall-way. She was a little taller, and a little thinner, and her nose was different, but she was so like Nellie, it was hard to believe. I'd never seen this girl before – she was a complete stranger to me, and yet I felt as if I had known her for a long time. I felt as if we were friends. I had to stop myself from running over and hugging her.

Maeve was delighted with my reaction. 'No,' she said. 'It's not Nellie. It's Johanna. I told you they were like twins.'

'Johanna,' I said. 'Nellie is going to be so happy to see you. She's only gone downstairs this very minute. I'll go and get her, or you can come with me and ...'

Johanna didn't move or smile or anything. She

stood and stared at me and her cross face reminded me a bit of what Nellie used to look like when I first arrived at Lissadell, before we were friends.

Now Lady Mary stepped forward. 'Johanna is tired after the journey,' she said. 'And perhaps a little over-whelmed. Johanna, why don't you sit for a moment and catch your breath?'

Lady Mary opened the door of a small room and led Johanna inside. Then she turned back to me and Maeve.

'Give Johanna five minutes to rest, and then go and fetch Nellie.'

Then she closed the door leaving Maeve and me outside in the hall.

* * *

'You've got to tell me everything,' I said. 'Tell me every single thing that happened today.'

'Well, we only have five minutes, but I'll do my

best. When we got to Temple House, Aunt Mary told Mrs Perceval the whole story, and she sent for Johanna, or Susan, as she called her. When she said her real name was Johanna, Mrs Perceval looked embarrassed, even though it wasn't really her fault.'

For a second I was angry. 'Johanna wasn't so far away – why didn't she ever come looking for Nellie? Didn't she have any idea how sad and lonely she was?'

'She thought that Nellie was dead. She was told that both her sisters died of the fever when they were little.'

Tears came to my eyes as I thought how bad some people were, how they could tell such cruel lies to a poor girl who had already suffered so much.

Maeve continued her story. 'When Aunt Mary told her that Nellie was alive and well, Johanna started to cry, and it was sad and happy at the same time and I wanted to cry too.'

'So how did Johanna end up coming here? Has Lady Mary invited her to stay for the night? That

would be so nice for Nellie.'

'That's the very best bit. Mrs Perceval is going to stay with her sister in London for a few weeks, and she hadn't planned to bring Johanna with her.'

'And Lady Mary needs a lady's maid!'

'Yes. At first Mrs Perceval said Johanna could come and work in Lissadell for a few weeks, while she was in London, and then go back to Temple House.'

That was both good news and bad. The sisters could be together for a while, but what would happen when they had to part?

Then Maeve continued. 'Aunt Mary was great. She talked about how hard it would be if the girls were separated again, and Mrs Perceval surrendered. She said she'll find a new maid when she comes back from London – so here we are. Johanna is staying here with us at Lissadell.'

I'd miss helping Lady Mary dress in the evenings, but this was a better result than I could ever have dreamed of.

Come on,' I said. 'Let's go and tell Nellie the wonderful news.'

Chapter Sixteen

'Wake up, Nellie. Wake up.'

Nellie jumped out of bed, and reached for her uniform that was neatly folded at the end of her bed.

'Oh, no!' she said. 'You're dressed already, Lily. Why didn't you wake me? Mrs Bailey will ...'

She stopped talking when she saw that Maeve was standing behind me.

'I don't understand,' she said. 'Is it morning? What's wrong?'

'It's still night-time,' I said. 'And nothing's wrong. We're here because ... oh, Nellie, it's Johanna – Maeve and Lady Mary found her. She's come to work at Lissadell as Lady Mary's maid. Your sister is alive and well and she's ... she's here.'

I expected Nellie to jump up and down with joy, but that didn't happen. She seemed puzzled, looking

around the small room as if Johanna could somehow be hiding somewhere.

'She's upstairs,' said Maeve. 'With Aunt Mary. Come on, Nellie. Don't you want to see her?'

Nellie walked towards the door and then stopped and looked down at her old, faded nightgown. 'I can't go upstairs like this,' she said. 'Let me get dressed.'

After all these years, I didn't think Johanna would care what Nellie was wearing, but I'd never been in a situation like this before, and I didn't know what was right or wrong. I handed Nellie her Sunday dress, which was also old and faded, and helped her to button it up.

She pulled on her stockings and boots, and then I realised that it was important to me that Nellie would look her best, so I grabbed my hairbrush from my locker, and ran it through Nellie's beautiful red curls.

'Ready?' I asked.

Nellie gave a small nod, and like a girl in a trance,

she followed Maeve and me upstairs.

* * *

As the three of us stood outside the small room, I could hear Lady Mary's voice, soft and soothing, as if she were talking to a little child. If Johanna was answering her, she was speaking so quietly I couldn't hear her words.

'Here we are,' I said. 'Ready?'

'I'm scared,' said Nellie.

I tried to put myself in her shoes. If I'd been away from Winnie and Anne for years and years, and was now separated from them by a single wooden door, I'd run in and kiss and hug them until they begged for mercy. But what could I know? How could I ever understand all the things Nellie and her sister had been through?

'Will you come in with me?' asked Nellie.

I took her hand in mine. 'Of course I will. I'm right

here by your side.'

Maeve opened the door and the three of us walked in. Lady Mary was seated in the only chair, and Johanna was looking out the window into the darkness, almost as if she wanted to escape.

Lady Mary stood up. 'Nellie,' she said. 'This is your sister Johanna.'

For a minute, no one moved or spoke. Then Johanna took one step forward, and held out her hand.

'Pleased to meet you,' she said, in a voice exactly like Nellie's.

'And you,' said Nellie, taking the hand, shaking it briefly, and dropping it as if it were burning her. Then they moved apart.

'Have you been well?' asked Johanna.

'Yes, I have. What about you?'

'I have been well too. Thank you.'

I looked at Maeve.

What was going on?

Why were these two girls acting so stiff and polite

– as if they were strangers?

This should have been the happiest moment of their lives – so why did they both look so terrified and lost?

They stared at each other for a long time, like two girls made of stone.

And then Nellie started to cry. Big fat tears rolled down her cheeks and she didn't even try to wipe them away. Her sobbing was the saddest, loneliest sound I had ever heard.

'JoJo,' she whispered. 'JoJo.'

Lady Mary stood up and moved towards Nellie, but before she got there Johanna came to life. She ran the few steps across the room and threw her arms around her sister. Even though they were almost the same size, she somehow picked her little sister up, and carried her to the chair. There she sat down with Nellie on her knee. Nellie continued to sob as she clung to Johanna and buried her face in her neck. No one else moved as Johanna stroked her hair, and

began to rock from side to side.

'They told me you were dead, Nellie,' whispered Johanna. 'If I had known you were alive, I would have come for you. I would have walked the roads of Ireland until I found you. I'm so sorry. I promised Mam I would take care of you always, but I didn't do it.'

'They were terrible times,' said Lady Mary. 'And you were only a child yourself. None of it was your fault.'

It was hard to tell if Johanna had heard her, as she continued to rock. And then she began to sing in a beautiful sweet voice. I couldn't make out the words, but I could tell they were Irish. As Johanna sang, Nellie relaxed a little, and slowly her sobbing became less.

Johanna rocked and sang for a long time, while the rest of us watched with tears in our eyes.

In the end, Lady Mary patted Nellie's shoulder. 'We will leave you two girls alone for a while,' she

said. 'Feel free to stay up here for as long as you like, and when you're ready, you can go downstairs to bed.'

Then she turned to Maeve and me.

'I think you two girls should go to bed also. Lily, maybe it would be best if you slept in Teresa's room. Nellie and Johanna should be together tonight.'

'Of course, Lady Mary,' I said.

I followed Lady Mary and Maeve out into the hallway. I watched as they went up the grand staircase, and then I went to the narrow servants' stairs and made my way to bed.

* * *

Teresa's room was bigger than mine and Nellie's, (which was right, as it was a room for a lady's maid, and Nellie and I were only housemaids). Also, I had it to myself, as since Lady Georgina moved out, there had only been one lady's maid at Lissadell.

I found it cold and lonely. I had never before slept

in a room on my own, and I didn't like it.

As I lay in the darkness and thought about how happy Nellie must be, I couldn't help feeling a little sorry for myself.

I missed the sound of Nellie's quiet breathing beside me. I was used to being everything to her. Being nice to her made me feel good about myself, but maybe I wasn't ready to share her.

Would everything be different from now on?

Would Johanna be the one to comfort Nellie when she was sad?

Would Johanna want to take over Nellie's reading lessons?

Would I always have to sleep alone, while Nellie and Johanna chatted in their room, sharing secrets that didn't include me?

Chapter Seventeen

'Lily.'

I opened my eyes and everything seemed strange. I was in Teresa's bed, and Isabelle was sitting beside me – and it was almost daylight!

'I'm so late,' I said, throwing back the blankets and jumping up. 'I'm going to be in big trouble. Where's my uniform and—?'

Isabelle laughed. 'It's all right, you don't have to rush. Mrs Bailey told me everything that happened last night, and she said that you and Nellie deserve a little rest after all the excitement. You and Miss Maeve should be proud of yourselves. Imagine finding Nellie's long-lost sister – it's like a fairytale come true.'

'It was so wonderful,' I said. 'And I'll tell you all about it later, but now I have to get dressed. It's late,

and there's so much to do. I've got to do the drawing room and the dining room and ...'

'Don't worry, Delia has already done the downstairs rooms. Mrs Bailey said she won't do as good a job as you and Nellie would, but that it will be all right for one day. She says you can take your time getting dressed, and when you're ready you can do the dressing rooms as usual.'

'And Nellie and Johanna?'

'You're to wake them as soon as you're ready. Nellie is to work as usual, and Johanna is to report to Mrs Bailey, to get instructions for the day. Now I have to go. The little ones will be awake soon, so I have to prepare their baths and get their clothes ready. See you later.'

* * *

I opened the door of my own bedroom, and tiptoed inside to see the sweetest sight in the world. The sis-

ters were in Nellie's bed, all curled up together, with Johanna's hand resting lightly on Nellie's cheek.

'Nellie,' I said quietly. 'Time to wake up.'

Nellie opened her bright blue eyes. For a second she looked confused, but when she saw Johanna lying beside her, a huge smile lit up her face.

'She's really here!' she said. 'I woke in the night but I was afraid to open my eyes in case it was all a dream.'

Now Johanna's eyes opened too. It was almost scary, how alike these two girls were. She gave Nellie a quick kiss on the cheek and climbed out of bed.

'Good morning, Johanna,' I said, as she began to dress. 'I hope you slept well.'

Johanna stared at me – not in a friendly way.

'When you're ready, you're to report to Mrs Bailey,' I said. 'She's going to tell you what to do for the day.'

'You don't have to order me around,' she said. 'I know what I have to do. Lady Mary told me last night.'

'I wasn't ordering you around. I was only—'

'Sounded like an order to me.'

Her voice was cold, and for a minute I hated her. Did she know how hard Maeve and I had worked to get her here? Did she know how much her presence meant to Nellie?

'I was asked to give you a message,' I said. 'And that's what I did. It wasn't an order.'

Johanna shrugged. 'What do you think, Nellie?'

Nellie didn't answer as she looked from her sister to me and back again. I wanted her to take my side, but how could she argue with her sister on their very first day together?

'I'll see you in a minute, Nellie,' I said. 'Delia has done the downstairs rooms and we're to get started on the dressing rooms.'

Then I hurried away.

* * *

As we worked that day, Nellie didn't say much about Johanna. I knew she was embarrassed by her behaviour, but didn't want to be disloyal.

Sometimes though, Nellie hummed or sang, and I knew that she was happier than she had been for a very long time.

At dinnertime, we met Johanna at the door to the servants' dining hall. We were a little late, so most of the staff had already taken their places. I was about to go to my seat when I turned back to Johanna. Even though she hadn't been very nice to me, I felt sorry for her. I remembered my first day at Lissadell, when I had no idea where to sit, no idea that places were ranked according to how important your job was. At the time I thought that was unfair, but now I was glad about it. Nellie and I could sit together as always, while Johanna would sit further up the table, closer to Butler Kilgallon. But what if Johanna didn't know that? Would she try to sit beside Nellie, and would everyone laugh at her?

'Johanna,' I said. 'There are special places for us to sit. You have to go—'

'I am not an imbecile,' she said sharply. 'I have worked in a big house before and I know perfectly well what to do.'

I didn't know whether to cry or laugh. Why was this girl being so mean to me when I had done nothing mean to her at all?

* * *

Nellie went to bed before me that night. Twenty minutes later I walked along the servants' corridor. I didn't know where to go, though. My things were in the room I had always shared with Nellie, but was that my room any more?

Did Johanna want to take my place?

I didn't want to do anything to make that grumpy girl happy, but if it were to make Nellie happy too, that was a different thing altogether.

Should I not make a fuss?

Should I make things easier for everyone?

Should I take my things and move them to Teresa's old room?

While I stood in the corridor unable to make up my mind what to do, Mrs Bailey came out of her office.

'Ah, Lily,' she said. 'I've been meaning to talk to you all day. I wanted to congratulate you. That is such a kind thing you and Miss Maeve did, bringing those two sisters together.'

'Thank you, Mrs Bailey.'

'Now off to bed with you. I believe you had a late night last night and you must be tired.'

Even though Mrs Bailey was sometimes cross with me, I knew she had a kind heart, and at that moment I had no one else to talk to.

'Mrs Bailey,' I said. 'I don't know what to do. I don't know where to sleep.'

'You will sleep with Nellie, as you always have.'

'But what about Johanna? She slept in my room last night, and I thought ...'

'Johanna will sleep in Teresa's old room. That's where the lady's maid always sleeps.'

They were the exact words I wanted to hear – but then I remembered how sweet Nellie and Johanna had looked in bed that morning. I remembered how Mam always told me to be kind, above everything else.

'If Johanna wants to sleep in my room from now on, I don't really mind. I can sleep very well in Teresa's room.'

Mrs Bailey smiled at me. 'You are a sweet girl, Lily,' she said. 'And I know that's not what you really want.'

'But ...'

'Lily, dear, bringing Nellie and Johanna together is wonderful, but things might be difficult for a while.'

'Why? Being together is all those girls ever wanted.'

'You are right, but they have been apart for so very long, and things can't change overnight. Trust me,

child. These girls have much to work out, and they will need a little space to do so. Things won't be easy, and things won't be perfect – not yet.'

I didn't fully understand what she was trying to say, but I could see she was busy and I didn't like to ask any more questions.

'Thank you, Mrs Bailey,' I said, wondering what I would do if I got to my room and found Johanna all tucked up in my bed, cuddling my doll, Julianne, taking my place.

'You are welcome,' she said, and then, as if she could read my mind, she added one more thing. 'And don't you worry. I have spoken to Nellie and Johanna about this and they understand the arrangements. Sleep well, child.'

Chapter Eighteen

The next morning, when I was finished cleaning the upstairs bedrooms, I met Isabelle, who was walking along the corridor holding Bridget by the hand. Bridget was normally a placid little girl, but she was whining and wriggling and didn't seem at all happy.

'Oh, dear,' said Isabelle. 'This little one is such a crosspatch today. Nothing I do will get her to settle. I even promised her I'd bring her outside to see Michael's seal, which usually works like magic, and that didn't help.'

'Hello, Bridget,' I said. 'Are you the best girl in the house?' Bridget cried and turned away from me, making me feel a bit foolish.

'Don't worry,' said Isabelle. 'That's the way she has been all morning.'

Then Johanna came out of Lady Mary's bedroom and came over to us. I smiled to myself – surely Johanna's grumpy face would make Bridget cry even more.

But Johanna knelt down in front of her. 'Hello, sweet girl,' she said. 'That's a very pretty dress. I think you must be the most lovely girl in all of Sligo.'

And to my surprise, Bridget gave her a huge smile, and reached out and took her hand.

'I'm Bridget,' she said. 'And I'm nearly three.'

'Such a big girl!' said Johanna. 'I thought you were four at least. My name is Johanna. Can you say that? Jo…hanna?'

'JoJo,' said the child proudly. Then, clearly loving the sound, she repeated it over and over again. 'JoJo. JoJo. JoJo.'

It was a very sweet moment, but suddenly Johanna stood up and ran away towards the back stairs. Isabelle shrugged, showing she had no idea what was going on either. I ran after Johanna, so confused for a

moment that I forgot I was supposed to hate this girl.

'Bridget liked you,' I said as I caught up with her. 'Why did you run off like that?'

Johanna turned towards me and I could see the tears in her eyes.

'JoJo,' she said, and then I remembered.

'That's what Nellie called you, isn't it?'

'And Lizzie too, when they were little and couldn't say "Johanna", and now ...'

'Oh,' I said. 'I'm sorry. That must be sad for you. That must remind—'

But then it was as if she became a different person. Her face became hard and cold. 'What do you know about sad, with your mam and your brothers and sisters all happy together?'

'I'm sorry for all the bad things that happened to you, truly I am,' I said. 'But it's not my fault my family is happy – and anyway, we've had our hard times too.'

She ignored me. 'And you think you're so great, hobnobbing with Miss Maeve and Lady Mary,

acting as if you were equals. You make me sick to my stomach and I don't know how Nellie can stand to be near you every day.'

I ran down the stairs with tears in my eyes. Johanna was being so mean, and so unfair. All I ever wanted was to make Nellie happy, and now I was afraid I had brought a monster to live and work with us.

* * *

For the next few days I stayed away from Johanna as much as I could. If she wanted to be mean to me, that was fine, but I wasn't going to make it easy for her.

Occasionally I passed her as I went about my work. A few times I saw her on the upstairs corridor. Often little Bridget was trailing after her, chattering and laughing. Once I saw Johanna bend and hug the little girl, before turning away and going back to her work.

* * *

One evening I went to the nursery to return the books Nellie had finished reading, and to get some new ones for her.

'Shhh,' said Isabelle when she saw me. 'We have to whisper. Bridget has finally fallen asleep and I don't think I could bear it if she woke up again.'

'But she's so sweet,' I said.

'She's a perfect darling,' said Isabelle as she knelt in front of the bookcase. 'But she has me worn to a frazzle. If I take my eye off her for one second, she vanishes and I have to search everywhere for her. That's not easy in a house as big as this.'

'Where does she go?'

'Looking for Johanna.'

I made a face. 'Why would she want to do that?'

'Johanna is nearly always nice to her.'

'*Nearly* always?'

'Sometimes she ... oh, I don't know – it's almost as if she can't bear to see her. Luckily, when that happens I can distract Bridget so she doesn't notice.

Mostly she's nice though – and Bridget loves her.'

'But ...'

'Maybe Bridget sees something in Johanna that we can't.'

'Like what?'

'Kindness?'

'I'm doing my best, but mostly all I can see in that girl is meanness.'

'You poor thing,' said Isabelle, putting her arm around me. 'I know none of this is easy for you.'

'It's not. I'm afraid that bringing Johanna to Lissadell was a huge mistake.'

'Here,' said Isabelle, handing me a big bundle of books. 'Let's hope that it will turn out like these stories, and Nellie and Johanna will live happily ever after.'

* * *

On Thursday, it was Nellie's day off, and I felt my

usual jealousy as I got dressed while it was still dark, and she could stay curled up all cosy in her warm bed.

'What are you going to do for the day?' I asked.

'You know – the usual. I will go for a walk by the sea, and I'll do some reading and mending.'

'And what about Johanna?'

'She has to work today and next Thursday, but Lady Mary said that after that, Johanna can have Thursdays off, so we can spend the day together. I'm looking forward to that so much.'

'That's nice,' I said, thinking that a whole day with Johanna wouldn't be much fun.

I sat on Nellie's bed. 'Dear Nellie,' I said. 'Is Johanna nice to you? Is having your sister back as good as you dreamed it would be?'

Nellie gave a big long sigh. 'I love Johanna. I love her so very much, but ...'

'You can tell me anything,' I encouraged her.

'It's hard. Sometimes she can't stop kissing me and hugging me. She looks at me as if she's afraid I'm

going to vanish into thin air, and that that would be the worst thing in the world. But ...'

'But?' I helped her.

'But sometimes, she's cold and mean. Sometimes she snaps at me, and says cruel things. Sometimes she looks at me and it's as if she doesn't care if she ever sees me again in her whole life. It's scary and confusing.'

I didn't know what to say, or how to comfort her. Why couldn't Johanna be the perfect sister Nellie deserved?

I leaned over and put my arms around her. 'I'm sorry,' I whispered. 'I'm sorry having her back isn't the way you had hoped.'

Then I went to pick up my brush and mop, ready for another long day.

* * *

'Oh, Mam,' I said, trying not to cry, as she threw her

arms around me and gave me one of her lovely hugs. 'I've never been so glad to see you in my whole life.'

'My poor little pet. Bring the bicycle in and tell me all about it.'

It was Saturday again, and I was so very happy to be home. I propped the bicycle against the kitchen wall, and after we'd all had a kiss and a hug, Mam chased the little ones into the yard to play.

'Well,' said Mam when the two of us were settled in the kitchen. 'Tell me what has made my lovely girl sad.'

So I told her the whole story (leaving Maeve out of it) and Mam listened the way she always did, sometimes nodding or sighing, but never interrupting.

'And now I don't know what to do,' I said. 'I don't know if Nellie was better off before Johanna came back into her life. I know *I* was happier before I met that cross, snappy girl. Sometimes I wish I'd minded my own business, and done nothing at all.'

Mam smiled. 'You're a very kind girl,' she said. 'You

always want to make things better for everyone, so doing nothing was never going to be your choice.'

'But what if I made things worse for Nellie?'

'Ah, pet, it's very early days yet, and what you say reminds me of something.'

'What's that?'

'Remember you told me that when you first met Nellie, her behaviour was confusing to you?'

'Yes. It was terrible. I couldn't decide if she was a nice girl or a horrible one.'

'And as you got to know her, you learned more about all the sad things that had happened to her. You understood that she was afraid of being close to you, afraid that she might lose you, and afraid of the pain that would cause. She was pushing you away, so she wouldn't get hurt.'

'Yes, I remember now – and I'm so glad I didn't give up on her.'

'It sounds as if those two girls have had a very difficult time of it.'

Then I remembered something else, and told Mam how Johanna was sometimes very sweet with little Bridget, and how sometimes she could hardly look at her.

'The poor darling,' said Mam. 'Didn't you say that Johanna was the oldest of the three sisters?'

'Yes,' I said crossly. 'The oldest and the meanest.'

'Be nice.' Her two simple words made me ashamed. 'Sorry, Mam.'

'Can't you see, pet? That poor girl felt responsible for the younger ones. She was trying to be mam and dad to them, when she was still only a child herself. When they were all sent to the workhouse, she blamed herself. Seeing little Bridget must bring all those dark days back – those days when no matter how she tried, she couldn't save her sisters. She thought they were both dead, and she has lived with that guilt on her young shoulders for so many years.'

'That must have been horrible.'

'I'm sure it was. And now she has found one of her

sisters alive and well, and that brings joy and pain. She's grieving for the little one they lost, and trying to come to terms with seeing her baby sister nearly all grown.'

'Oh, Mam. Everything makes so much sense when I'm here with you, but when I go back ...'

She hugged me. 'Be as nice as you can to that poor girl, and if she's moody, try to be patient, try to under-stand. Things will get better, I'm sure of it.'

Winnie and Anne raced into the room. 'We're tired of playing on our own,' said Anne. 'Come with us, Lily. Come play with us.'

Mam smiled. 'Off you go,' she said. 'And be back in time to help me with the dinner.'

* * *

'Nellie? Are you awake?'

'I am now. What do you want?'

'I talked to Mam today, and I think I understand

things a bit better. Remember when I came here first?'

'I don't like thinking about that. I wasn't very nice to you.'

'That's true, but later I understood why. You told me about losing your mam and daddy, and your sisters and your friends. I know you were afraid of losing me too.'

'I remember now. I didn't want to be hurt any more.' Her voice was so quiet I could just about hear her. 'Do you think maybe Johanna is a little bit afraid?'

As she said the words, I knew they were true. 'Yes, I think she's afraid, and she's feeling guilty too. None of what happened was her fault – but she feels she should somehow have protected you.'

'Oh, Lily, your mam is so wise. I'm sorry I said Johanna was mean. She's not mean at all, is she?'

I was wondering if maybe Johanna was a little bit mean, when I thought of something else – (and I felt proud that it was all my own idea, and not Mam's!)

'Nellie, you know how your life here in Lissadell is

so important to you?'

'Lissadell saved me. It's my home now. Without Lady Mary's kindness ...' She stopped talking for a minute, and I knew she was figuring it out for herself. 'Do you think Johanna misses Temple House?'

'Yes,' I said. 'I think maybe she does.'

'Thank you for helping me to understand.'

'You're welcome.'

'Poor Johanna. I think we should both be extra-kind to her from now on.'

I smiled to myself in the darkness. Nellie was a better person than me, and she didn't know how hard a thing she was asking.

Chapter Nineteen

In the days that followed, things slowly got better. I learned to smile and walk away when Johanna was mean to me, and sometimes she was, well, maybe not nice, but *almost* nice.

Then one afternoon, Nellie and I were mending sheets when Johanna came in with a jewellery box in her hand. Nellie beamed when she saw her, and made space on the seat beside her. I felt a whisper of fear for my friend. Which Johanna were we going to see today?

'These necklaces of Lady Mary's are all tangled up,' said Johanna as she sat down next to Nellie. 'Little Bridget has been meddling with them. Lady Mary was cross with her at first, but I said Bridget didn't mean it. She is such a sweet little girl, she would never deliberately spoil them.'

I smiled. Johanna and Bridget were the best of friends these days, and everyone smiled when they heard Bridget running along the landing, saying 'JoJo. Where you go, JoJo?'

'Anyway,' said Johanna. 'Lady Mary has asked me to untangle these. It's going to take me hours.'

I thought untangling fine gold chains would be more fun than mending endless boring old sheets, but I didn't say anything.

Nellie and I had been talking about my last visit home, but now I didn't want to continue the conversation. I never knew what was going to set Johanna off, and make her say mean things to me.

Then Johanna turned to me. 'There's something I've been wanting to say to you, Lily,' she said.

I didn't dare to speak. I stared at her, doing my best to stay calm, repeating Mam's advice silently to myself. *Try to be nice. Try to be patient*

'It's about Nellie.'

'What about her?' We were talking about Nellie as

if she wasn't sitting right next to us, but I didn't know how to stop Johanna without sounding rude.

'You've been very kind to her. You've been a good friend.'

I was so surprised, I wasn't sure what to say to this.

'And you've been helping her with her reading – that's such a wonderful thing to do.'

'I was happy to help,' I said, smiling at Nellie. 'She's so clever, it wasn't hard at all.'

Then I thought of something else. There was no easy way to say it, so I blurted it out. 'When you were in the workhouse in Tubercurry, Johanna, did you ... did you go to school? Because if you didn't, I'd be happy to ... you know ... help you to ...'

For a while, Johanna didn't answer, and I wondered if I had offended her. Just when she was being nice to me, had I managed to ruin everything?

'I was lucky,' she said in the end. 'Well, not exactly lucky, because the workhouse I was in was horrible – all workhouses are terrible places – but in Tubercurry

the teacher was kind, and I learned to read and write and do my sums.'

'I'm sorry,' I said. 'I mean, I'm not sorry you had a kind teacher, I'm very happy about that. I'm sorry if you're insulted because I thought ...'

And then Johanna laughed, and I had never heard her laughing before, and it was the most beautiful sound, and even though what I said wasn't all that funny, I laughed too, and so did Nellie, and the three of us laughed for a long time.

After that, we chatted a bit, but mostly we worked in silence. It wasn't an awkward silence though, it was the warm silence between friends, when you're comfortable together, and there's no need to say anything at all.

* * *

I was yawning and pulling on my stockings when Nellie jumped out of bed.

'What are you doing?' I asked. 'It's Thursday. You don't have to get up. You can stay in bed for the whole long day if you like.'

'I don't want to stay in bed. I want to enjoy every minute of this special day.'

And then I remembered.

'I nearly forgot,' I said. 'This is Johanna's first Thursday off. What are you two going to do for the day?'

'I don't know,' said Nellie. 'And I don't care! Oh, Lily, you were so kind to bring me home that time with you, but except for that day, I've always been alone on my day off. I've always been glad of the rest, but sometimes … sometimes it has been lonely.'

I hugged her and then quickly put on my boots, ran my hairbrush through my hair and put on my frilly white cap. 'I'm so happy for you both,' I said. 'And I hope you have a wonderful day together.'

* * *

When I finally got back to my room that night, Nellie and Johanna were sitting on Nellie's bed. At first they didn't see me, as I stood at the door, enjoying the happy scene. Nellie was reading aloud from one of the nursery storybooks, and I felt proud as she managed every single word, with barely a stumble.

Johanna clapped her hands as Nellie came to the end of the last page, and I joined in.

'Lily,' said Johanna, looking up. 'Isn't Nellie such a great reader now? And you must be a very good teacher.'

She was being kind, but her words made me feel sad. Was I ever going to be a real teacher?

'Did you two have a lovely day together?' I asked.

'It was perfect,' sighed Nellie. 'We walked to the sea and had a paddle until the cold turned our toes blue, and then we went in to the village, and Johanna bought me this ribbon.'

It was a small, narrow scrap of green ribbon, nothing like the fancy ones Bridget wore in her hair, but I

could see that to Nellie it was precious beyond words.

'That's lovely,' I said. 'And what else did you do?'

Nellie turned to her sister. 'Will we tell her?'

'Better than that, let's show her. Put on your coats, girls, it's cold outside.'

* * *

As we walked through the servants' tunnel, Johanna held the lantern Harry had given her high over her head.

'Be careful, girls,' she said. 'Don't trip – look there's a bumpy patch of ground there – and mind your heads on the low bit.'

I smiled to myself. Johanna was taking her duties as a big sister very seriously, and Nellie didn't seem to mind at all.

'Where are we going?' I asked. 'It's dark, and it's cold and we should all be in bed.'

'Not far now,' said Nellie. 'Just at the other side of

the apple-drying house.'

'I don't want an apple,' I whined. 'I want my bed – and anyway, I heard cook saying the last of the apples are rotten by now.'

'We wouldn't bring you out in the dark to give you a rotten old apple, Lily,' said Johanna. 'Just be quiet and follow us and you will see what we have done.'

Nellie reached out and took my hand, and I knew she was trying to say sorry for Johanna's sharp words. I squeezed her hand to show it didn't matter. Nellie was glowing with happiness these days, and a few sharp words was a small price to pay for that.

Nellie held her hands over my eyes as we walked around to the back of the apple-drying house.

'It's so dark I can't see much anyway,' I said, but she only laughed.

She guided me for the last few steps, and I could hear the scraping sound as Johanna set the lantern down on a stone.

'Ready,' she said.

'Look, Lily,' said Nellie, taking her hands away from my eyes. 'Look what we have done.'

It took a second for my eyes to adjust to the flickering light from the lantern, and when I finally made out what was in front of me, I felt like crying.

Nellie and Johanna had cleared a patch of grass and weeds between some trees, and laid a circle of smooth flat stones on the earth. Inside the stone circle were three bunches of wild flowers tied up with string, and three large white stones. As I leaned closer, I could see that there was a single word on each of the white stones – *Mam Dad Lizzie*

'Oh,' I gasped. 'That is perfect.'

'We don't know where they are buried,' said Johanna. 'And we wanted somewhere we could go to remember them – somewhere nice with trees and grass, as they all loved nature and birds and plants and things.'

'It took us ages to find the stones we wanted,' said Nellie.

'And Albert gave us paint to write the names,' said Johanna.

'And I did some of the writing too.'

'And Lady Mary said it was all right to do this.'

'And she said we can have some of Sir Josslyn's special daffodil bulbs to plant in the autumn, and some other things too, so there will always be flowers here, and we will always have a special place to remember our lovely family.'

It was a sad and a happy moment all mixed up together. I hugged them both, and as the three of us walked arm in arm back to our beds, Nellie leaned over and whispered in my ear. 'Thank you, Lily. Thank you so much.'

Chapter Twenty

a few days later, Lady Mary came to the dining hall and called me out to the corridor. Everyone stared as I got up from my chair and followed her. One of the kitchen boys made a face at me, as if I were in a lot of trouble, but I made a worse face back at him. For the first time, I didn't feel nervous or guilty about talking to Lady Mary. I knew she liked me, and I was confident I hadn't done anything wrong.

'Lily,' she said, when she had closed the door. 'I wonder if you could do something for me?'

'Of course, Lady Mary,' I said. 'Is there something you would like me to mend?'

'No. It's about the needlework school. The assistant, Miss Flanagan, has been called away suddenly. Her mother has been taken ill.'

'I'm sorry to hear that, Lady Mary.'

'Some new women have joined the school today, and there is an order to fill, and Miss Connor cannot possibly manage on her own.'

Already my mind was racing away. What was she saying? Could she possibly mean ...?

'Would you like me to ...? Am I to go over there and help to finish some of the garments?' I blurted out. 'Oh how I would love to do that! I promise I would do my very best work, and ...'

Lady Mary smiled at me, and for a second I feared I had made a terrible mistake. Was she going to go back to Sir Josslyn so the two of them could laugh at how uppity I had become?

'That would be an option, I suppose,' she said gently. 'And it is very kind of you to offer, Lily, but—'

'That's all right,' I said. 'I understand. It was silly of me to even dream. My mam says I shouldn't get notions about myself.'

Lady Mary put up her hand to stop me talking.

'I was thinking that you could be assistant to Miss Connor this afternoon. I know you are young, but I am sure you would be very well able. All you would have to do is—'

'Me?' I knew I shouldn't interrupt her, but I worried I hadn't heard her properly.

'Yes, you, Lily,' she said. 'I think you would do a very good job. Now go there directly, and Miss Connor will give you your instructions. I will talk to Mrs Bailey, and explain where you have gone.'

I wanted to kneel down and kiss her hand. 'Lady Mary,' I said. 'Thank you so much.'

'No need to thank me. You are the one who is doing a favour for me. Now run along. Miss Connor is waiting for you.'

I began to walk along the corridor towards the back door, but she called me back. I turned, wondering if this was all some joke that wasn't even very funny.

'You might want to leave your apron and cap in your room,' she said. 'This afternoon you won't be a

housemaid, you will be a needlework assistant.'

* * *

I practically floated all the way to the coach house courtyard. My head was about to explode from excitement. Wait till Mam heard about this. She would be so proud of me.

Then I got to the bottom of the stairs leading up to the school, and for the first time, I began to feel nervous. I held the wooden handrail tightly, resisting the urge to turn and run away.

What if I didn't know what to do?

What if I made silly mistakes?

What if everyone laughed at me?

Then I remembered what Daddy used to say to me when I was little – *Work hard, Lily, and you can do anything or be anything your heart desires.'*

I'm not stupid. I knew I couldn't become a princess or a doctor or something like that. Maybe even

becoming a school teacher was an impossible dream, but I knew I could do what Lady Mary had asked, and I knew how proud Daddy would be if he could see me. So I breathed deeply and took the first step.

* * *

Once again, the school was warm and cosy and friendly. Three or four groups of women sat together in different parts of the room. Miss Connor smiled when she saw me, making me a little less nervous.

'You must be Lily Brennan,' she said, coming towards me and shaking my hand. 'Lady Mary and Lady Georgina speak highly of you, so I am very happy to have you here.'

'Thank you.'

'Now let's not waste time with chatter and I'll show you what you are to do. I will be working with the experienced women, and you can assist the new-comers.'

She took me to a corner of the room, where five women were sitting around a small table.

'This is Miss Brennan,' she said.

'Hello, Miss Brennan,' they chorused.

Now I felt embarrassed. Why were they calling me 'Miss?' They were all much older than me, and one even looked older than my mam.

'Hello,' I said quietly.

'Miss Brennan might be young,' said Miss Connor. 'But she is a genius with a sewing needle. Now, Miss Brennan, take a seat and you can get started.'

I knew how to sit down – I'd been doing that on my own since I was a tiny girl, but after that what was I supposed to do?

'You'll work it out as you go along,' said Miss Connor, as if she could read my mind. 'These new women are practising their hemming stitches. Your job is to guide them – and those stitches need to be invisible – I will be putting on my strongest glasses to check!'

As Miss Connor walked away to another group, one of my women rolled her eyes, making me feel a little bit better.

'We are working on scraps of fabric for the moment,' she said. 'But when our stitches are good enough we will be moving on to hemming christening robes.'

And all of a sudden, I knew I could do this job. Mam had taught me how to do perfect hemming when I was only five or six years old. I was going to show Lady Mary that she had made a good choice. I was going to be the best needlework assistant Lissadell had ever seen. I sat down and picked some fabric and a needle and thread from the table.

'This is the way I find easiest,' I said, and all of the women laid down their fabric and watched me sew.

* * *

The time flew by. The women chatted as they worked, telling stories about their homes and their families.

I told them about my mam and brothers and sisters
and how far away they were, and one of the women,
Mary-Kate, gave me a big hug and called me a poor
little pet.

After a while, I held out the piece of fabric I had
been working on, and everyone looked at it closely.
Then I examined at their work. Some of it was quite
good, but not yet as good as mine.

'I've been hemming since I was a girl,' said Mary-
Kate with a big sigh. 'I've been making dresses for
my children since they were babbies – and as long as
it held together and kept them warm on a winter's
day, we were all happy. Here it's different – knowing
Miss Connor is going to check my work makes me
nervous.'

'I know,' I said. 'My friend Rose used to start shaking when our teacher, Miss O'Brien examined her
work.'

'And this material is so fine and light,' she said.
'It makes me feel all clumsy – and the silk thread –

sure it's hardly even there at all – it's like sewing with something invisible.'

So I sat beside her for a while, showing her how to make her stitches smaller, tucking the thread under the hem as she moved her needle along the fabric.

At five o'clock, Miss Connor came over. I felt nervous as she went from woman to woman, examining what they had done. I wondered if this was how the Master felt when an inspector used to come to our school.

'I am impressed,' said Miss Connor. 'This is very good work.'

'She's a goodly little teacher,' said one of the women, smiling at me.

Miss Connor held up four pieces of fabric. 'Whoever did these may move on to hemming a christening robe tomorrow,' she said. Then she held up a fifth piece – Mary-Kate's work.

Suddenly I remembered sewing classes from when I was at school. Miss O'Brien loved Hanora and me,

because our sewing was so good, but with Rose it was a different story. Once Miss O'Brien hit Rose on the knuckles and threw her sewing into the bin. If I'm ever a real teacher, I won't do things like that.

'Mary-Kate did her very best, Miss Connor,' I said quickly. 'And I think she's getting better. I'm sure that by tomorrow her stitches will be perfect – she only needs a bit more practice.'

Miss Connor smiled at me. 'That's exactly what I was going to say, Miss Brennan,' she said. 'Now you'd better get back to the house and I will see you tomorrow.'

I didn't understand. 'But ...?'

'Didn't Lady Mary tell you? Miss Flanagan will be away until Saturday, at the very least. You are to help me here tomorrow afternoon and the next afternoon also, and after that we shall see what happens. Now run along, or I will be in trouble with Mrs Bailey.'

'Yes, Miss Connor,' I said. I was trying to sound calm, but inside, I was jumping up and down. I didn't

want to wish harm on Miss Flanagan's mother, but I couldn't help hoping that she'd stay sick for a little while longer.

* * *

As I hurried along the basement corridor I met Nellie, who ran over and gave me a big hug.

'What was it like at the sewing school?' she asked. 'How was the needlework? Was it very exciting? Was it hard? You're so good at sewing that probably didn't matter. What did you have to do? Did they like you? Can you go back again some time?'

I laughed, loving how excited she was for me. 'It was very nice,' I said. 'And I can go back for two more days at least. Well, in the afternoons anyway, in the mornings and evenings I'll be doing my usual work here with you.'

Just then Maeve came along, carrying a big bundle of songbooks. Nellie and I stopped talking – it was

hard to get used to seeing one of the family in the basement. It was hard to remember that even though there were so many strict rules, Maeve usually did exactly as she liked.

'Hello,' she said. 'I want to give you these song-books from Ardeevin, Nellie. I know I promised them to you ages ago, but I'm afraid I forgot.'

'Oh, Miss Maeve,' said Nellie. 'It is so kind of you to think of me. Johanna is a lovely singer, so I am going to share these with her.'

Nellie hurried off towards Johanna's room with the books, but I was happy to see that Maeve looked as if she was settled in for a long chat. I hadn't seen her for ages, and I missed her.

At first we talked about Nellie and Johanna, and Maeve was pleased when I told her how well they were getting on.

'And what about you, Lily?' she asked. Have you been having a nice time here while I was stuck at Ardeevin with horrible old Miss Clayton?'

She always asked me things like this, and I couldn't help feeling a bit cross. Maeve was great fun and she could be very sweet and generous, but our lives were different in so many ways. She could never understand how I wished I could spend whole days reading and doing sums and learning geography.

I wanted to tell her about my afternoon at the needlework school, but I stopped myself. I knew she'd be polite, but she would never understand how important it was to me. Since she'd never had a job in her life, how could she understand the difference between a lovely one, and one I only did to help to buy food for my family?

Maeve was my friend, but sometimes I felt as if she and I were staring at each other from the top of two tall mountains. We could wave and talk, but could we ever truly be close to each other?

* * *

At the end of my third day in the needlework school,

Miss Connor called me to her desk.

'Lily,' she said. 'I want to tell you how pleased I am with your work. All the women love you, and you have been an excellent teacher to them. Their work has improved greatly since you arrived.'

'Thank you,' Miss Connor,' I said.

'I have received a message from Miss Flanagan.'

'Is her mother still sick?' I asked, trying not to sound too hopeful.

'Unfortunately her mother is still very unwell.'

'I'm sorry to hear that.' It was half true. Miss Flanagan's mother was probably a nice lady, but ...

Did I dare to hope?

Could it be that Miss Flanagan wasn't coming back?

Could it be that Miss Connor wanted me to take her place?

But then all my hopes faded away.

'Luckily for Miss Flanagan,' continued Miss Connor. 'She has five sisters, and they are all able to

help out so that Miss Flanagan can return to us at Lissadell.'

I put my head down so she wouldn't see the stupid tears that had come to my eyes. 'I'm happy for her,' I said.

Then Miss Connor put her arm around my shoulder. 'I can see that you like it here, Lily,' she said. 'And I am sorry you cannot stay. Don't worry though. You are young and you are bright. You will find your place in the world.'

Now the tears flowed down my cheeks. What if my place in the world was to be always far away from my family, doing a job that bored me almost to death?

* * *

But soon afterwards something terrible happened – something that made me realize that a boring life is not the worst thing in the world.

Chapter Twenty-One

'Oh, Lily,' said Nellie, when I got to our room after a long day. 'Johanna and I have had the most perfect day together. We walked to the village and we even had tea and cake in a tea-room – like real ladies. I was afraid to go in at first, but Johanna said it would be all right – and it was. I love my days off with her. I wish every day could be Thursday.'

'I'm glad you had a nice time,' I said, pulling off my boots and throwing myself onto the bed. 'I could tell you about mine, but it would send you straight to sleep. First I cleaned the fireplaces, and then …'

Nellie lay back on her bed and gave a big fake snore, and we both laughed. Just then there was a knock on the door.

'Mrs Bailey wants to see you both in the servants' hall,' said Maggie.

'It's late,' I said. 'Why would she want to see us at this hour?'

'I don't know,' said Maggie. 'But it's not only you two. She's asked to see all of the household staff. There's something going on, but don't ask me what it is.'

She hurried on to the next room, and I slowly put my boots back on to my sore, swollen feet.

* * *

Mr Kilgallon and Mrs Bailey were both in the dining hall – standing with their hands clasped in front of them and looking very serious. I had no idea what was going on, but I could tell that it wasn't good.

Most of the servants were already lined up in two rows. Usually the dining hall was a place full of chat and laughter, but now no one was speaking. Some people looked confused and some looked tired. Nellie and I went and stood next to Johanna and Isabelle.

They both nodded at us, but no one smiled.

Ita, the scullery maid came running in, with her boots unlaced and her hair still tied up in rags. 'Sorry, Mrs Bailey,' she said. 'I was so sound asleep, I couldn't drag myself out of my dreams. I ...'

She stopped talking when she saw the rows of silent servants. 'Sorry,' she whispered again, and went and stood next to the kitchen maids.

'That is everyone,' said Mrs Bailey. 'Please close the door, Harry, and then we may proceed.'

Even Harry, who was usually all smiles, looked serious as he went to close the door.

I felt sick.

What was happening?

What did Mrs Bailey want to proceed with?

Had someone died?

Were the Gore-Booths moving away and closing up the house for good?

Were we all going to lose our jobs?

Mr Kilgallon took a step forward. 'I apologise for

bringing you here like this,' he said. 'But something terrible has happened.'

All around me, it was as if everyone was holding their breath, waiting for Mr Kilgallon's next words.

'Something very valuable has disappeared,' he said.

I felt like breathing a big sigh of relief. I didn't own anything valuable, and I hadn't made anything valuable disappear. I wished he'd hurry up with his little speech, so I could go to bed.

'What is it?' asked Ita. 'What's gone missing?'

Mr Kilgallon glared at her, but Mrs Bailey answered the question. 'It is a very precious gold locket belonging to Lady Mary. She is quite certain that it was in her jewellery box this morning, and now it is no longer there. We have searched her room, and have to conclude that it has been stolen.'

Now I could hear gasps from the other servants. We had all heard the stories of people in big houses who had been sacked because of theft. Times were hard in the country, and many of us had families who

needed our wages. Which of us would risk our good jobs for a gold locket?

'Oh, my,' said Ita. 'Are the police on their way?' At the mention of police, some people went pale, and Delia began to cry. I knew I hadn't done anything, but I couldn't help feeling guilty anyway.

'The police have not been called ... yet,' said Mr Kilgallon. 'I ask you all to stay here while we conduct a search of your rooms. You may sit if you wish, but please do not leave the dining hall.'

And then he and Mrs Bailey walked out of the room.

* * *

As soon as the door was closed the whispering began.

Nellie, Johanna, Isabelle and I went to sit together at the end of the big table. Nellie was holding tightly to her sister's hand.

'Poor Lady Mary,' I said. 'That locket was very

special to her.'

'Save your pity for whoever took it,' said Isabelle. 'Their life in Lissadell is over now – and their life in service too.'

'What do you mean?' I asked.

'Anyone who's sacked for stealing will leave without a reference – and without a reference they'll never again get a job – or not a decent one anyway.'

'Serves them right,' said Johanna. 'Whoever did this is causing trouble for all of us.'

Nellie didn't say anything. She always hated fuss and bad feeling.

Then I noticed that two of the kitchen maids were staring at Johanna. They were sitting at the other side of the table, but I could hear little bits of their whispered conversation. '... the only new person here ... always in Lady Mary's room ... lots of chances to ... bad breeding ... workhouse ...'

I remembered what Nellie had told me, how often other servants were suspicious of ladies' maids, never

sure if they could be trusted. Was Johanna going to suffer because she was new, and because she spent so much time with Lady Mary?

I wanted to run over and shake the whispering girls, and tell them that Johanna would never steal, that just because she spent time in the workhouse, that didn't mean she was a bad person.

But I didn't dare to do anything – I couldn't let Nellie know what they were saying. So instead I glared at the kitchen maids until they began to talk of something else.

* * *

Much later, Mrs Bailey and Mr Kilgallon came back into the room, and the nervous whispering stopped.

'We have found the locket,' said Mrs Bailey, holding it up for us to see. It swung from her fingers, and twinkled in the glow from the gaslights. It seemed like a very small thing to be causing such a big fuss.

'You may all go to your rooms,' she said, and people began to get up, muttering about how late it was, and how tired they were. Then she continued. 'Except you, Johanna. Would you please come with us? Lady Mary is waiting for you upstairs.'

Now the muttering got louder and louder. The kitchen maids were standing right in front of me and I heard one of them saying ' I knew it ... can always tell bad blood – Ow!!'

She turned back to look at me, but I was busy admiring the Latin writing on the large beam running over our heads – and pretending I hadn't pulled her hair sharply.

Johanna had gone white, and looked as if she were going to faint.

'It wasn't me,' she whispered. 'I didn't take it. I'd never steal. It's wrong.'

Mrs Bailey came over. 'Come along, Johanna,' she said. 'Let's not make things even worse.'

'I didn't do it,' said Johanna. 'I swear it wasn't me.'

Mrs Bailey took Johanna's arm, but Nellie held on to the other one. Nellie had a fierce look in her eyes, a look I had never seen before, a look that made me a little afraid. But I knew that if she didn't let go, she was going to be in trouble too

'It's all right, Nellie,' I said. 'I bet this is all some kind of mix-up. Let's go to our room, and when everything is sorted out, Johanna can come back and tell us all about it.'

Slowly Nellie let go of her sister, and allowed me to lead her to our room.

We put on our nightgowns, but I knew we wouldn't sleep until we saw Johanna again. Nellie came to my bed, and I wrapped Mam's shawl around the two of us.

Nellie sobbed and sobbed in my arms. 'It's a mistake,' she said. 'I know it's a mistake.'

'Of course it is,' I whispered. 'Try not to worry. Lady Mary is fair and decent. She'll sort everything out.'

It was very late when Johanna came to our room. She was still pale, and her eyes were red from crying.

Johanna sat on Nellie's bed, and Nellie ran over and curled up beside her.

'Tell us everything,' I said.

'They found the locket under my bed,' said Johanna. 'They said it was in the old biscuit box where I keep Mam's bible, and Daddy's pipe. But I didn't put it there. I never touched it – well, I did often, when I was tying it on Lady Mary's neck – but I never took it. I wouldn't do such a thing. Stealing is wrong.'

'And did Lady Mary believe you?'

Tears came to Johanna's eyes. 'No. She didn't believe me. She kept saying she understood, that I had so many changes in my life, and how hard things were for me. She said I probably borrowed the locket, and meant to put it back tomorrow. I could see that Mrs

Bailey didn't agree with that, but Lady Mary kept on talking anyway. I told her a hundred times I hadn't taken the locket, and she kept not believing me.'

'So now?' I asked.

'Nellie's right when she says Lady Mary is a saint. She believes I took her locket, but she still wants to give me another chance. She said if it happens again, I will have to leave Lissadell, but if it doesn't, she's prepared to forget all about it.'

I knew Johanna was innocent, but I still couldn't help feeling that she was lucky Lady Mary hadn't called the police. If the police had come, they would never have believed Johanna's story.

'Well that's not so—' I began.

'That's terrible,' she snapped. 'Lady Mary says she is giving me a second chance, but that's not fair – I haven't used up my first one yet – and I never would. I know how lucky I am to have this good job, and to be with Nellie. I would never, ever do anything to spoil that.'

'I know,' I said. 'I believe you.' It was the truth. Poor Johanna had lost the rest of her family, and being with Nellie was the most important thing in the world to her.

'I haven't been sacked,' she said. 'But now everyone here thinks I'm a thief.'

'Lily and I don't,' said Nellie fiercely.

Johanna gave us a sad smile. 'Thank you,' she said. 'But that's not enough. From now on, everyone will be staring at me, waiting for me to take something else. My life is ruined.'

Nellie cuddled closer to her sister, but I couldn't stay still. I jumped out of bed and began to walk up and down the small room.

'I don't understand,' I said. 'We know you didn't take the locket, Johanna, but how did it end up under your bed?'

'Magpies often take shiny things,' suggested Nellie.

'I know, pet,' said Johanna gently. 'But they don't bring them into houses. They don't hide them in

boxes under beds.'

'So who did it?' I asked. 'Who would do that to you?'

'No one ever really trusts lady's maids,' said Johanna. 'We all know that's true.'

'Maybe,' I said. 'But no one would do that to you just because you're a lady's maid.'

'I suppose whoever did this really hates me, then,' said Johanna.

'That would make sense,' I said. 'Except no one hates you.'

I knew this was true. Johanna had been snappy when she first arrived, but that often happened when new servants came to Lissadell. Who knew what terrible lives they were escaping from? People understood this, and were ready to give second chances. Even the gossiping kitchen maids never meant any real harm. They would never try to ruin someone's whole life like that.

I gave a big yawn, and I couldn't help thinking

251

about how close it was to morning, and how little sleep I would be getting that night, and how cross Mrs Bailey was going to be about all the fuss.

'I'm going to bed,' said Johanna suddenly.

'You can sleep here with me if you like,' said Nellie.

'That's all right, darling,' said Johanna. 'I don't want to act as if I'm guilty. I am going to act as normal.'

Then she kissed her sister on the cheek and held her head high as she walked from the room.

Poor Johanna. I wondered how she could be so brave, but then I remembered that she'd had a terrible life, and this was far from the worst thing that had ever happened to her.

Chapter Twenty-Two

Next day, when Johanna came into the servants' hall there was a bit of pointing and whispering, but Mrs Bailey marched to the top of the room and put on her sternest face.

'Has anyone got something they would like to say?' she said.

No one said a word.

'Hmm, that's what I thought,' said Mrs Bailey. 'There's no one in this room who's perfect, and that's for certain sure.'

Johanna took her place, but she didn't touch her food. I smiled at her, but I couldn't tell if she even saw me, as she sat there in silence.

* * *

As the days passed slowly by, and nothing else went missing, people began to talk about different things.

One day I went into the small room off the kitchen where Harry ironed the newspapers. I did this whenever I could, as I loved to hear what was happening in the big, wild world outside Lissadell.

'What's the news, Harry?' I asked, as I sat on a stool in the corner of the room. 'Is there anything I should know about?'

He laughed as he held the paper towards me. 'There's a lot here about the Irish Citizen Army,' he said.

'Has that got something to do with Countess Markievicz?'

He smiled. 'Sometimes it seems that she is part of every group in Dublin. I believe she's still well in with the Volunteers and Cumann na mBan and the Fianna, but she's very big with all the Citizen Army crowd too, to be sure. I hear it said she's their treasurer, and she's been out to Lucan and Clondalkin

trying to gather followers to the cause.'

I had heard of the Citizen Army, of course, but still I was shocked. It was very hard to imagine the glamorous countess being part of a real army.

'Tell me all about them, Harry,' I said. 'You always know more about these things than I do. Is it a real army with uniforms?'

'Oh, yes, it's a real army. I believe they have ordered dark green uniforms from Arnotts – very posh I'm sure.'

'And are women like the Countess – are they allowed to fight?'

'They are allowed and encouraged,' he said. 'They drill alongside the men, as if they were equals.'

'And have they got guns?' I whispered the words, almost shocking myself.

'Some have rifles and some have sticks. Knowing the Countess, though, I expect she will have got herself a rifle.'

This was so exciting! It was hard to imagine the

fine lady I knew marching in a real army with a gun and a uniform. I could have sat there all day, chatting to Harry, but Mrs Bailey was calling for me, and I didn't want to be involved in a small battle all of my own.

* * *

When I went to sweep the library later, I was surprised to find Maeve there.

'Oh,' I said. 'I thought you were at Ardeevin.'

'I was supposed to be, but Gaga was coming here for the night, so I escaped with her. Miss Clayton will be so cross when she realises I'm not there.'

'For someone who has escaped, you don't look very happy.'

'I'm not,' she said, holding up the newspaper. 'Gaga tries to keep me away from the news, but she's not very good at it.'

I smiled. If Maeve wanted to do something, it was

very hard to stop her.

'Have you seen this?' she asked.

'Er, I think I might have. Was it on the tray Harry was carrying upstairs?'

I wasn't sure if the family knew that many of the servants read the daily newspaper before it made its way up to the drawing room.

'There's a story about Mother here,' she said. 'As usual.'

'Really?' I said, trying to sound as if this was news to me.

Maeve gave a big sigh. 'My friend Stella's mother is often in the newspaper too.'

'Well, that's all right then, isn't it?'

'Not really. Stella's mother is famous for attending garden parties, and going to fashionable balls. What my mother does is ... very different.'

I felt sorry for her. Saving Ireland was all very well, but Maeve was paying the price for that. Even when she was surrounded by people, she had a lonely, sad

air about her.

'Anyway, enough about Mother,' said Maeve, crumpling the newspaper and throwing it onto a table. (I couldn't help thinking how Harry would have to iron it all over again.) 'I heard what happened with Johanna. Do you think she really took Aunt Mary's locket?'

'No!' I said, shocked. 'She definitely didn't.'

'Sorry,' said Maeve. 'You know her better than I do, and if you say she didn't do it, then I believe you. At least it's all over now, though.'

'That's the trouble. It might not be over at all.'

'What do you mean?'

'Someone tried to make Johanna look like a thief, and they might do it again. Lady Mary is very kind and gentle, but if that happens, she will make Johanna leave Lissadell, and then ...'

Maeve didn't argue with me, and knowing she thought I was right didn't make me feel any better.

'So how can we help her?'

'All we can do is keep an eye on Johanna's room, in case anyone else goes in there.'

'We can take turns,' said Maeve. 'We'll be like characters in a Sherlock Holmes story.'

'That's the trouble,' I sighed. 'This isn't a story, and neither of us can spend our days hanging around the servants' rooms. I spend most of my time cleaning upstairs, and you're at Ardeevin more often than not.'

'So what are we going to do?'

'All we can do is hope and pray that nothing happens. If Johanna has to leave, then Nellie ...'

I couldn't even finish the sentence. The thought of Johanna leaving Lissadell and Nellie, was too sad.

* * *

'Ouch!' I cried. 'That's the second time I've stuck the needle into my finger.'

'You poor thing,' said Johanna. 'Do you want me to bandage it?'

'Thank you, but I think I'll live,' I said, smiling. Often Johanna acted as if she were my big sister too. Sometimes it annoyed me, but mostly it was very sweet.

It was a few weeks after the incident with the locket, and everyone was beginning to relax a little. Johanna had got into the habit of coming into our room for a while before bed, and I found myself looking forward to these quiet moments with the two sisters

'How is the dress coming along?' asked Nellie.

'Sewing on velvet is harder than I expected,' I said. 'But I think I'm getting the hang of it now.'

I spread the half-made dress on the bed beside me and stroked the soft red fabric.

'That's beautiful,' said Nellie.

'I agree,' I said. 'But the green is even nicer. It reminds me of a forest on a sunny day, so that's the one I love the most.

'So how did you decide which colour to give each sister?' asked Johanna.

'Anne is older, so she is getting the nicer one – the green,' I said.

'But that's not fair,' said Nellie. I smiled. Nellie was getting used to the idea of being a little sister again.

'Actually it *is* fair,' I said. 'Because when Anne gets too big for the green dress, it will be passed on to Winnie – she will have a chance to wear both.'

'That's clever,' said Nellie.

I picked up my sewing again, and Johanna opened one of Maeve's song books.

'Here,' she said to Nellie. 'Let's try this one.'

Nellie read the words with only a little help from her sister, and then the two of them began to sing softly. I closed my eyes and listened to their beautiful singing. I knew these were special moments I would remember for the rest of my life.

Chapter Twenty-Three

'Where were you, Johanna?' said Nellie sleepily a few days later. 'Lily and I were almost asleep.'

'Sorry,' said Johanna, pulling off her shoes and throwing herself onto Nellie's bed. 'Lady Mary went away to visit her sister this afternoon. She asked me to tidy her wardrobes while she is gone, so I decided to make a start. That woman has so many clothes I could be working for a week and never be done.'

'I'm too tired now for reading or singing,' said Nellie. 'Do you mind if we put the light out and chat for a while?'

No one argued with this, so when the light was out, Johanna snuggled under Nellie's covers, and I listened as they talked about their plans for their next day off together.

I was almost asleep when the door opened and I could see Isabelle's head peeping in.

'Lily, Nellie,' she whispered into the darkness. 'Have you seen Johanna anywhere? She's not in her room.'

I could hear Johanna sitting up in bed. 'I'm here,' she said. 'What do you want?'

Isabelle opened the door fully, and in the light from the corridor I could see her worried face.

'Mrs Bailey wants to see you in her office immediately,' she said.

Now I sat up too. 'What could be so urgent that it can't wait till morning?' I said.

'No idea,' said Isabelle. 'Sorry.'

Nellie lit the gaslight, and I watched as Johanna straightened her apron and cap and put on her shoes. She looked worried. I knew all four of us were thinking the same thing, though none of us dared to say it.

'I'll go with you,' said Nellie.

'There's no need,' said Johanna. 'I haven't done any-

thing wrong. You stay there in bed and I'll be back in a minute.'

Johanna hurried from the room, and Isabelle sat on the edge of my bed. Nellie sat in her own bed looking looked pale and worried.

'Do you think ...?' she began.

'I'm sure there's nothing to worry about,' I said, not feeling sure at all.

As the long minutes passed, I was glad that Isabelle had stayed with us. Something big was happening, and I didn't know if I could handle it without her. No one talked as we waited. Nellie was picking at the edge of her blanket, and I knew she was going to ruin it, but that didn't seem important.

And then Johanna came back.

* * *

Johanna was sobbing so much, it was difficult to understand what she was saying. Her shoulders

shook as she hugged Nellie fiercely. Isabelle and I stood helplessly next to them. We didn't need to hear the words to know what had happened.

When Johanna was calmer she let go of her sister and told us everything.

'When the valet went to lay out Sir Josslyn's dressing table tonight, he saw that his best silver comb was missing. He told Mr Kilgallon, and he and Mrs Bailey went to my bedroom while I was upstairs in Lady Mary's room.'

I closed my eyes, and wanted to block my ears too. I was afraid to hear the next words.

'They searched under my bed,' said Johanna. 'And they found the comb in my old biscuit box – but I didn't put it there. I never touched it. I've never even seen it. They must think I'm so stupid. They warned me I had no more chances, so why would I steal something and hide it in my own room, in the very place they were going to look first?'

Tears rolled down Nellie's pale cheeks, but she

didn't say anything. Isabelle held my hand, but she too was silent.

'I believe you, Johanna.' I said. 'But now what's going to ...?' I didn't know how to finish my question.

'Mrs Bailey said I have to go,' she said. 'I have been dismissed, and I must leave Lissadell.'

'Now? You're leaving now? In the dark?' I said. 'Mrs Bailey can't!'

Johanna shook her head. 'She said I may sleep here for one last night, but I have to go after breakfast in the morning. She said I will be paid what I am owed. She thinks she is being fair and generous, even though she is being so wrong, and so cruel!'

'We'll have to talk to her,' I said. 'We'll have to make her understand.'

'I tried,' said Johanna as tears came to her eyes again. 'I tried and tried, but she won't listen to me. I know I'm lucky she didn't call the police but ... I didn't do anything wrong. I didn't take the stupid comb.'

I jumped out of bed, and began to pull on my uniform. 'We can't let this happen,' I said. 'Someone else has done this, and you can't be punished for it. I'll go and talk to Lady Mary. She'll listen to me. She won't let this happen.'

'But Lady Mary is away, remember?' said Isabelle. 'And who knows when she will be back.'

'Maeve,' I said. 'I'll talk to Maeve – she will know what to do.'

'I have to go back to the night nursery, in case the children wake up,' said Isabelle. 'I will walk as far as Miss Maeve's room with you.'

* * *

When I woke Maeve she didn't delay. As she followed me down the back stairs I began to feel a bit hopeful. Mrs Bailey liked Maeve, and was usually prepared to break all kinds of rules for her. Surely she would listen to her now.

When Maeve knocked on the door of Mrs Bailey's office, I waited in the corridor out of sight.

'Come,' said Mrs Bailey in a tired voice.

Maeve went into the room and I could hear as Mrs Bailey stood up from her desk, clearly surprised to have a member of the family appear in the middle of the night, barefoot and dressed only in her night-gown and a fine satin wrap.

'What is it, Miss Maeve?' she said. 'Are you unwell? Has there been an accident?'

'It's about Johanna,' said Maeve. 'I don't think she took Uncle Joss's comb, or Aunt Mary's locket.'

'Dear girl,' said Mrs Bailey. 'Those things were found in her bedroom.'

'I think someone else took them, and is trying to blame Johanna.'

'All the other household staff have been here for quite a while – and everyone came with excellent references,' said Mrs Bailey. 'None of them would do anything like this, of that I am perfectly sure.'

'I'm going to talk to Uncle Joss,' said Maeve. 'He'll believe me, I know he will.'

'I have already mentioned it to him,' said Mrs Bailey. 'He does not have time to interview everyone concerned, and he is happy to leave the matter in my hands. Lady Mary trusts me with the care of the household, and I cannot break that trust.'

'But ...'

'I am sorry for Johanna, but as you know, there are many valuable things in this house, and it is my duty to protect them. I don't like this part of my job, but that does not mean I can walk away from my responsibilities. The decision has been made, and it will not be changed.'

'But Johanna didn't do it,' said Maeve. 'I *know* she didn't.'

'I'm afraid this is what comes from being too friendly with the servants, Miss Maeve,' she said. 'You don't understand how they are different to you.'

'I understand that Johanna didn't do anything.'

'That girl comes from a very troubled background. She has never had nice, valuable things in her life, and I suppose she found it hard to resist. Life is cruel, and she is to be pitied, but she cannot stay here after tomorrow.'

'What is she to do, and where is she to go?'

Now Mrs Bailey spoke in a gentler voice. 'I'm afraid that cannot be my problem. I am truly sorry for the girl, which is why I am not calling the police. I will make sure she leaves with enough money to keep her for a little while. That is the best I can do. I suggest that you return to your bed, and allow me to handle things from here.'

Maeve was too well brought up to stamp her foot or shout, so she walked from the room and only closed it with the littlest of slams.

'I'm sorry,' she said to me. 'There's nothing I can do.'

* * *

When I got back to my room, Nellie and Johanna looked at me hopefully. They had trusted me to make everything right, but I hadn't managed to do anything at all.

'I did my best,' I said. 'But it didn't work. Mrs Bailey has made up her mind, and there's nothing we can do to change it. I'm sorry, Johanna.'

Nellie started to cry again. 'I'll go with you, JoJo,' she said. 'I can't stay here without you.'

Now Johanna stood up tall. 'You are *not* to do that, Nellie, do you hear me? I will be perfectly fine. I can find myself somewhere to stay in Sligo until I find a new position.'

'But who will employ you without a letter of recommendation?' asked Nellie.

It was a good question and I didn't know the answer.

'Something will work out,' said Johanna bravely. 'It always does. Now I had better go and pack my

things.'

Nellie was still crying. 'Will you come back and sleep here with me – one last time?'

'Of course I will,' said Johanna. As she wiped away a tear, I realised she was not at all as brave as she was pretending to be. She was putting on an act for Nellie. She was still trying to protect her little sister.

Chapter Twenty-Four

In the morning, though neither of had slept at all, Nellie and I had to get up as usual to clean all the downstairs rooms and the family dressing rooms. Johanna stayed in bed, as though this were one of her days off.

When I was fully dressed, Nellie was still slowly tying her boot laces.

'Hurry up,' I said. 'We're already late, and I know how you like to be on time in the mornings.'

'This isn't any old morning,' said Nellie. 'I didn't want this morning to ever come, and now it has, and ...' Once again tears began to roll down her face.

'Pull yourself together, Nellie,' said Johanna. 'And stop making a fuss about this.'

I could see that she was pretending to be cross, but Nellie quickly finished tying her boots and hurried

to the door.

'That's a good girl,' said Johanna. 'You have a fine job here at Lissadell and you don't want anything to spoil that.'

'But what about you?' asked Nellie.

'To tell the truth, I was a little tired of being a lady's maid,' said Johanna. 'Times are changing you know, and there are more things a young woman can do.'

I thought maybe Johanna could get a job as an actress, since she was doing such a good job convincing Nellie that she didn't care about leaving Lissadell.

'You won't leave before …?' asked Nellie.

'No,' said Johanna. 'I won't leave before you come down for breakfast. Mrs Bailey said I can have breakfast here, and that's what I intend to do. Now hurry along, or you'll be in trouble.'

* * *

I had to do most of the work that morning, as poor

Nellie fumbled and tripped and dropped things.

'What will I do without her?' she repeated. 'What will I do without my JoJo?'

'I know it won't be the same, I said. 'But I will be here, and I will take care of you – and Johanna says she'll only go to Sligo, and that isn't so far at all, is it?'

But nothing I could say would make Nellie feel any better, so in the end we worked in silence. For the first time ever, I didn't want breakfast time to come.

* * *

Johanna was alone in the dining hall. Her small suitcase was on the floor beside her, with her coat neatly folded on top of it. Cook came in with a giant bowl of porridge and placed it in front of Johanna.

'I don't know what Mrs Bailey is thinking of,' she said, wiping away a tear. 'We all know you're as good a girl as ever worked here. Now eat up, and there's a slice of pie to follow. I'll make you up a little package

for your journey too.'

Nellie and I sat down on either side of Johanna, but when our food came, neither of us felt like eating. Johanna ate all of her porridge as well as a huge piece of pie – I suppose it's easier to eat when you don't know where your next meal is coming from.

Agnes, one of the kitchen maids came along to clear the plates.

'I'm sorry to see you go,' she said to Johanna. 'I know you didn't do it – and so do all of us kitchen maids – and we're sorry we believed it at first.'

I sighed. Was Mrs Bailey the only one who didn't believe Johanna? And why did she have to be the one with all the power to make her leave?

After that, the three of us sat in silence. Nellie lay her head on Johanna's shoulder, and Johanna stroked her hair. It was time for Nellie and me to go back upstairs to clean the family bedrooms, but neither of us moved.

After a while, Isabelle came and joined us. 'The

little ones are playing in the nursery,' she said. 'Nurse said she'd watch them so I can stay here with you for a little while.'

She was just another silent girl, but having her there made me feel a little bit better.

* * *

Before long, Mrs Bailey came into the room and handed Johanna an envelope.

'This is what you are owed,' she said. 'And there's a little extra to keep you going. I've also written down the name of a respectable boarding house in Sligo. Tell Mrs Fallon that I sent you. You will be safe there until you find another position.'

Johanna took the envelope, but she didn't thank Mrs Bailey. She didn't say a single word. She stood up, put on her coat, picked up her suitcase and walked towards the door.

If I had been in her position I would have kicked

and screamed. I'd have hung on to the legs of the heavy dining table and they would have had to drag me away. Johanna was very quiet and dignified though, and I had to admire her.

Suddenly Nellie ran to her sister, crying and sobbing. 'Don't go, JoJo. Don't go. Don't leave me again. I'll die if you leave me again!'

Tears came to Johanna's eyes, but she kept walking. I looked at Mrs Bailey, and saw that she too was close to tears. She didn't move though. She didn't say that Johanna could stay.

I looked at my friends and thought my heart was going to break. Then, without planning it in any way, I stepped forward and spoke.

'Don't make Johanna leave, because ...'

'Because what?' asked Mrs Bailey.

I took a long, deep breath. 'Because I'm the one who stole the things.'

Johanna stopped walking and Nellie stopped crying and Isabelle's mouth hung open in surprise.

Everyone stared at me.

'What are you saying, you foolish child?' asked Mrs Bailey.

'It was me,' I said. 'It was me all along. I am the one who stole Lady Mary's locket and Sir Josslyn's silver comb.'

'And why on earth would you do such a thing?'

'Because ... because ...' I didn't want to say the next words, afraid that Nellie and Johanna would hate me forever, but if I didn't say them, I knew Mrs Bailey wouldn't believe me. 'Because I was jealous of Johanna. I was jealous of how Nellie loved her the best. I was jealous of how they spent their days off together. I was jealous of how they sang together and laughed together. I was jealous of everything, and I thought if Johanna wasn't here, everything would be better for me – so that's why I hid the things in her room. I was trying to get rid of her.'

Mrs Bailey narrowed her eyes. 'Is this the truth you are telling me, Lily?'

I know lying is wrong, but if I really told the truth, Johanna would be out on the street, and Nellie would likely die of loneliness.

'Yes, Mrs Bailey,' I said. 'That is the honest truth.'

'I am very, very disappointed in you, Lily,' she said. 'I had you down as a good, kind person, and now I see how wrong I was. Doing such a cruel thing to an innocent girl is a terrible thing.'

I blinked hard at how unfair all of this was. I tried not to think of what my life was going to be like from now on. I tried not to wonder how I'd ever manage to get any kind of job without a reference. I held my head high as she continued to speak.

'I shall have to talk to Mr Kilgallon about this,' she said. 'All of you wait here until I return.'

Then she marched from the room.

Chapter Twenty-Five

I turned to Nellie and Johanna, ready for all the bad things they would say, but instead, Johanna came over and put her arms around me.

'What you are doing is wrong, Lily,' she said. 'You can't leave Lissadell. I know you didn't steal those things.'

Nellie didn't say a word as she ran to hug me too. I tried not to cry as those two, beautiful red-haired girls held me close.

'You didn't steal either, Johanna,' I said, pulling away from them. 'I agree that this is wrong, but if one of us has to leave, it should be me. I'll go and pack my things now, so I'll be ready when Mrs Bailey comes back. The walk home is long, and I might as well get started as soon as I can.'

I tried not to cry as I thought of Maeve's beautiful

bicycle. Never again would the village children clap and cheer and treat me like a queen as I cycled to see my mam. From now on I'd be a shame to my family – the girl who was sent home for stealing from the Gore-Booths.

'You can't do this,' said Johanna. 'I won't let you.'

'It's already done,' I said. 'I was always good at making up stories, and Mrs Bailey believes me. Nothing you say will make any difference now.'

'But—' Nellie and Johanna said the word together, as I pushed past them.

'Lily, wait!' said Isabelle, but I ignored her too and ran from the room.

* * *

I took my schoolbag from under my bed, and filled it with my few clothes, my prayer book and my hairbrush. I looked at my gorgeous doll, Julianne, a Christmas present from Lady Mary. Should I leave

that behind me? But then I decided I had done nothing wrong, and I deserved the doll as much as I ever had. So I put her into the bag, along with the half-made velvet dresses for my sisters – now I'd never have a chance to enter them in the home industries show. I looked around. When I first arrived at Lissadell I had cried many tears in that room, but now, in a strange way it almost felt like home. I had made many friends in this place, and had some very happy times. I loved Nellie and Johanna as if they were my very own sisters. I loved spending time with Maeve. I loved seeing Countess Markievicz, and listening to her interesting conversations. My time working in the needlework school had been so special, and now ...

I pushed the thoughts away as I tied the strap on the bag and took my coat from the hook behind the door.

'Goodbye,' I whispered as I stood in the doorway, saying farewell to the room, and the life I'd had there.

I heard footsteps, and Isabelle appeared.

'You're the kindest girl in the world, Lily,' she said. 'But you can't do this. You can't ruin your own life to save Johanna.'

'I can and I will. Don't you see, Isabelle? I have a family to take care of me, and Johanna has only got Nellie. I can't let them be torn apart again.'

'But what will happen to you? No one can get a good job without a letter of recommendation.'

'That's exactly why I should be the one to leave. I can go home to Mam and live with her again.'

'But the only reason you left home in the first place was because your family needed the extra money.'

This was true. I wasn't quite sure how my family would manage without my wages and the food Cook gave me to bring home every Saturday. Maybe I could grow more vegetables in our little garden, or take in washing? Maybe Molly Carty would pay me to clean out her henhouse every now and then?

But I knew it wouldn't be as easy as that. Now Denis and Jimmy would have to leave school early,

just as I did, and the thought of that broke my heart. Mam would go hungry again, sparing the best food for her children. Winnie and Anne would never have any more dresses made from the finest fabric in the land. All my lovely family was going to suffer, because of what I'd just done.

But still I knew I was doing the right thing. Nellie and Johanna had never had any luck until now. All they had was each other, and their jobs at Lissadell, and I wasn't going to let that be taken away from them.

'Mam will work something out,' I said. 'She brought me up to help others, so she will understand why I've done this.'

'And what about your dream of being a teacher?'

I could feel tears coming to my eyes. This was the hardest thing of all – after being dismissed for stealing, I had no chance of ever becoming a teacher. Who would ever believe in me? Who would ever trust me?

'That was never going to happen,' I said. 'That was

only a stupid dream.'

But everyone needs dreams, and I was trampling all over mine.

Dear Isabelle didn't want to give up. 'What if something goes missing again?' she said. 'What if another stolen treasure ends up in Johanna's room? Whoever did this hasn't gone away, and in a few weeks or months time, this could begin all over again – and you'll have given up your job for nothing.'

'I'm sure whoever did this will get such a fright, it will never happen again. I think it's over, Isabelle. When Mrs Bailey tells me to leave, that's what I'll do, and you can all get on with your lives. Now step out of my way and go back to the nursery, or you'll be in trouble too.'

'Who cares about the nursery,' she said. 'I'm staying with you until ... oh, Lily, you are so sweet and kind and funny, and I'm going to miss you very much.'

'Thank you,' I whispered. 'I'll miss you too.'

* * *

Nellie and Johanna were sitting in the dining hall holding hands. Nellie's eyes were red and puffy, and when she saw me, she began to cry again. Before anyone could say anything, Mrs Bailey came back into the room. She looked at my bag, and the coat over my arm.

'Are you sticking to the story you told me earlier, Lily?' she asked.

'It's not a story,' I said quietly. 'It's the truth.'

'Then you know I have no choice but to let you go. You must leave Lissadell immediately.'

I tried to be brave as I took a step towards the door.

'None of this is fair, Mrs Bailey!' cried Nellie. 'Don't make Lily leave. Please let her stay.'

'Are you saying Lily wasn't telling the truth?' I could see that Mrs Bailey was losing patience. 'Are you saying she isn't the thief?'

Nellie looked from me to Johanna with a pained

look on her face. She couldn't save both of us, but how could she possibly choose?

And then the door opened once more and little Bridget ran in, with Maeve a few steps behind her.

Bridget toddled over to Johanna with a huge smile on her face. 'JoJo,' she said. 'JoJo, I look for you. I look all the places for you.'

Johanna knelt down and hugged the child. 'I'm here, Bridget,' she said. 'You've found me now.'

Miss Bailey didn't look happy at this turn of events. 'What are you thinking, Miss Maeve?' she said. 'The child has no place down here. Please take her back to the nursery – or perhaps Isabelle, you could—'

But Maeve interrupted. 'What's going on, Lily?' she said. 'I know this isn't your day off, so why have you got your coat? Why are you carrying that bag? Where are you going?'

For one beautiful moment I thought Maeve could save me, but then I realised that saving me would ruin Johanna. If Maeve said I wasn't a thief, Mrs

Bailey would believe her, but then ...

'I ... I ...' I began a few times, but couldn't finish.

'None of this need concern you, Miss Maeve,' said Mrs Bailey. 'This is a matter for me and the servants. Please do as I asked and take little Bridget with you and go back upstairs.'

Now Maeve gave a huge smile, which made no sense to me at all. 'Of course, I'll take Bridget upstairs,' she said. 'But first, there's something I think you should see. There's something ...'

'Come, JoJo, come,' said Bridget loudly, trying to pull Johanna towards the door.

'This is turning into a circus,' said Mrs Bailey. 'And I won't have it. Please, Maeve!'

'Go with her, Johanna,' said Maeve, ignoring Mrs Bailey. 'And maybe everyone should see where they are going.'

So Johanna let Bridget pull her out of the room and along the corridor, with everyone else following along in a strange procession. At the door to Johanna's

bedroom, Bridget stood on tippy-toes and turned the door-knob. Then she pulled Johanna inside, with the rest of us squashing in behind them. Bridget knelt down and pulled Johanna's biscuit tin from under the bed. She held it towards Johanna, with a huge smile on her face.

'Surprise!' she sang. 'Bridget get surprise for JoJo.'

Johanna took the box from the child's hands, and held it away from her body, as if it were a bomb that could explode at any second. Then she lay it on the bed and opened the lid. Everyone leaned forward and for a long minute the room was silent. Inside the box was a bible, an old pipe ... and Lady Mary's pearls.

Chapter Twenty-Six

Bridget's smile slowly faded as she looked at all the faces gathered around her. She must have been disappointed with our reaction.

She took the pearls from the box and held them towards Johanna.

'Surprise!' she said again, but a little uncertainly this time. 'Bridget get present for JoJo.'

Now everyone spoke at once.

'Does that mean ...?'

'Who would have thought ...?'

'So none of the servants ...'

'Silence,' said Mrs Bailey. Her voice was quiet, but still everyone managed to hear her. She stooped down so her face was level with Bridget's.

'Did you put these pearls here?'

Bridget nodded happily.

'And where did you get them?'

'Mama's bedroom.'

'And why did you take Mama's pearls and give them to Johanna?'

The child looked around, as if the answer was easy. 'Mama has all nice things and JoJo has none,' she said.

I looked around the room, with its plain walls and bare floorboards and faded cotton curtains and wondered again at how unfair the world was. Even a tiny child like Bridget could see the difference between this simple place, and her mother's room, with its rugs and paintings and ornaments and satin cushions and velvet curtains.

'Bridget,' said Mrs Bailey. 'Did you get more surprises for Johanna before this?'

'Yes,' said Bridget, wrinkling her little face as she thought. 'I got her ... I got her a pretty locket ... and a shiny comb from Dada's room.'

Johanna picked her up and hugged her tight. 'You

sweet little girl,' she said. 'You were trying to be kind to me. How could you understand all the trouble you have caused?'

'Trouble?' said Bridget, looking worried.

'No,' said Mrs Bailey. 'You're not in trouble, but from now on, no more bringing surprises for Johanna, all right?'

The little girl nodded.

'Will I tell you what happened?' said Maeve, and without waiting for us to answer, she continued. 'I was coming downstairs to say goodbye to Johanna, and to say sorry that I couldn't ... well you all know about that, and I saw Bridget on the back stairs, and I couldn't quite see what was in her hand, but she looked very secretive, so I decided to follow her, and I watched as she went into Johanna's room, and put something into the biscuit box, and suddenly I knew for sure how the other things got there, so I told Bridget that Johanna was in the dining hall ... and you know the rest.'

'Isabelle, Isabelle! Where are you? Nurse is fit to kill you. The boys won't stop fighting and we can't find Bridget!'

It was the other children's maid, and she stopped suddenly when she saw the gathering in Johanna's bedroom.

'What's going on?' she asked. 'Why are you all here?'

'This has nothing to do with you,' said Mrs Bailey sharply. 'Isabelle, take the child and go upstairs at once. Maeve, please return the pearls to Lady Mary's room. Nellie, get a move on – do you think the bedrooms are going to clean themselves?'

Everyone hurried off. Mrs Bailey sat on the bed and put her head in her hands. Johanna and I looked at each other. What did this mean? Mrs Bailey was always strong, and in charge, so why did she now seem so old and so weak?

When Mrs Bailey finally looked up, I could see tears in her eyes. 'Girls,' she said. 'I hardly know what to say. I was doing my best to be a good, loyal housekeeper to

the Gore-Booths, and I made a mistake. I nearly did a terrible, terrible thing. I am deeply ashamed. Could I ask you both to accept my humblest apologies?'

I didn't know how to answer her. She was right. She *had* made a very big mistake. She didn't believe Johanna when she was telling the truth, but she did believe me when I was telling a lie.

But was it fair to blame Mrs Bailey?

What would I have done in her place?

If I hadn't known Johanna so well, I might have suspected her too.

While I was still working it all out in my head, Johanna spoke.

'That's all right, Mrs Bailey,' she said. 'I understand how this all happened, and I am grateful for your apology.'

'Thank you, dear,' said Mrs Bailey. 'How can I make it up to you both?'

My head filled with possibilities. Could we ask for a present? Extra pay? How wonderful it would be to

have a few days off to spend with my family.

But then Johanna showed that she was a much better person than me.

'There is no need for anything,' she said. 'Everyone makes mistakes.'

Now Mrs Bailey looked as if she wanted to hug her. 'That is very gracious of you, Johanna,' she said. 'But at the very least, I insist that you both join me in my sitting room for hot milk and a cake.'

* * *

I had only ever been in Mrs Bailey's sitting room when it needed cleaning, so it was very strange to sit on one of her armchairs with Johanna. It was very strange to be served by Mrs Bailey, watching as she stirred sugar into our milk, and handed us a plate of Cook's finest rhubarb tart with thick cream on top. It was very strange trying to make small talk about the weather, and how unusually cold it had been lately. It

was very, very awkward.

In the end, I was happy when Johanna drank the last of her milk, and got to her feet.

'That was nice, Mrs Bailey,' she said. 'But now I need to get back to work on Lady Mary's wardrobes.'

I jumped up too. Suddenly cleaning bedrooms with Nellie seemed like a wonderful thing to do.

'Thank you girls,' said Mrs Bailey. 'Thank you both very much.'

* * *

After that, Mrs Bailey was extra-kind to Johanna and me. Sometimes when I made a stupid mistake she was cross with me, but it was a gentle kind of crossness, as if she were giving out to a little child, or a puppy.

But in all the time I knew her, she never mentioned the incident again.

Chapter

Twenty-Seven

When Saturday came around, I cycled home as usual. It was early when I got there, and the street was quiet. In our little front garden, Mam was on her knees, planting flowers.

'Growing vegetables is important,' she always said. 'But having something pretty to look at is good for the soul.'

I wanted to ring the bicycle bell, announcing my arrival, but I hesitated for a moment. I watched Mam's reddened fingers making holes in the damp soil, and settling each plant in carefully. When she finished her work, she sat back on her heels, and gave a big happy sigh, and I was filled with love for her. Mam's skin was rough, and her hair was messy. Her

dress was so faded and patched it was hard to tell what colour it used to be. Still, to me, that woman kneeling in the dirt was worth a million of those fine ladies in Lissadell.

As I watched her, I dreamed of being a little girl again, living in that house where life was simple and Mam could make everything right.

'Mam,' I said. 'I'm here. I'm home.'

'Darling girl,' she said, as she stood up and wiped her muddy hands on her apron.

'I've missed you,' I said, throwing myself into her arms.

'And I've missed your smiling face too,' she said. 'How I wish I could see it every single day.'

'Oh, Mam,' I said. 'That nearly happened. Something very bad ...'

And then I started to cry.

'Sweet child,' said Mam. 'Sit down here on the bench with me and tell me everything.'

* * *

Mam didn't interrupt while I told my story, though a few times I saw the wrinkle on her forehead become deeper, and she twisted her hands together the way she always did when something made her worry. After a while, I saw that her eyes were watery, though I couldn't tell if that was from the cold wind. When I was finished talking, there was a long silence, and I began to worry. Had I been wrong in thinking she would understand?

'I'm sorry, Mam,' I said. 'Did I let you down? Are you disappointed in me? Did I nearly ruin everything for the whole family?'

She leaned over, and held my hand, squeezing it so tightly it hurt.

'My darling Lily,' she said. 'I have never been so proud of you as I am at this moment. I only wish your daddy were here to see what a fine young woman you're growing up to be.'

'So you're not cross?'

'No, pet. How could I be cross when you did such a good thing for your friends?'

'But if I lost my job?'

'Things wouldn't have been easy, but sure we've always managed before and we'd have managed again. Now let's go inside. The girls will be so happy to see you.'

* * *

When I got back to Lissadell, the sound of sweet singing coming along the basement corridor told me that Johanna and Nellie were already settled in our bedroom.

'There you are, Lily,' said Johanna who was sitting on my bed. 'Did you have a nice day with your family? I've picked some wild flowers for you, and put them on your locker.'

I smiled. There was barely any room on my small

locker, with the flowers she'd given me on Wednesday, the ribbon and comb she'd bought for me on Thursday, and the handkerchief Nellie had stitched for me on Friday.

'Thank you, Johanna,' I said. 'But ...'

'Don't you like them?'

I liked them very much. She'd arranged them carefully with leaves and ferns in a jam jar. That wasn't the point though.

'I love them,' I said slowly. 'I love all the things you've given me, but these last few days ...'

'What?' asked Nellie.

I didn't know if I could find words that wouldn't hurt their feelings.

'I miss you two,' I said in the end.

'But we're right here,' said Johanna. 'Thanks to you, we're both still here.'

'That's exactly it,' I said quickly. 'Before, we were equal – we were friends. Now you treat me like a queen or a princess or something. You bring me pre-

sents and make a fuss of me. I want to chat with you about other things. I want you to tease me and laugh at me, and act as if I'm just like you – but all you do is thank me – over and over again.'

'But—'

The two girls spoke together, but I held my hand up to stop them.

'In the end I didn't even do anything,' I said.

'You tried to,' said Johanna quietly. 'And that's what counts, but if you don't want us to thank you anymore, we won't.'

I smiled. 'Thank you. Now move over and let me sit down. My legs are killing me from all the cycling.'

* * *

After breakfast next morning I heard the sound of crying coming from the servants courtyard. I hurried outside and saw little Michael and Sir Josslyn.

'Spotty's too big for that pond,' said Sir Josslyn.

'It's not fair to keep him there any longer.'

Now that he said it, I could see it was true. We'd all got used to seeing the seal flopping around there, perking up whenever Michael appeared with fish treats, but I hadn't noticed how much the creature had grown.

'I'll make him a bigger pond,' said Michael, with tears streaming down his face. 'I'll get a shovel and dig and dig, until ...'

'He needs to be in the sea,' said Sir Josslyn gently. 'He needs to be with his Mama and Dada and his friends. I'll call the gardener and he can bring Spotty to the sea in his wheelbarrow.'

Then he turned around and saw me, 'Ah, Lily is it?'

'Yes, Sir Josslyn. Can I help?'

'I have an important meeting in a few minutes. Perhaps you could stay with young Michael until the gardener comes and then bring him back to the nursery?'

'Nooooo!' wailed Michael. 'I'm the one who found

Spotty on the beach, and I'm the one who should bring him back there.'

Sir Josslyn sighed. 'I suppose that is only fair,' he said. 'Lily I wonder if you would mind terribly?'

It was a beautiful sunny morning, and the thought of a walk to the beach sounded nicer than anything Mrs Bailey could have planned for me.

'Of course,' I said quickly. 'I'll go with Michael and the gardener, and then I'll bring Michael straight back to the nursery.' Before he could change his mind, I ran to the kitchen door. 'Tell, Mrs Bailey I'm doing an important job for Sir Josslyn,' I said to Delia who was at the chopping board. Then I ran back to Michael to wait for the gardener.

* * *

Spotty didn't seem to mind his journey in the wheelbarrow. Michael ran along beside him, talking all the time.

'You be a good seal for your Mama and Dada and your nurse,' he said. 'I hope they're not very cross with you for getting lost, but it wasn't your fault 'cause you were so small. Anyway, I think they'll be happy to see you again. They will teach you how to catch fish, 'cause when you're in the sea I can't feed you any more.'

When we got to the beach, the gardener lifted Spotty from the wheelbarrow and lay him on the sand. Spotty looked around and sniffed the air, and then he began to scoot and wriggle along towards the water.

'Goodbye, Spotty,' said Michael, and I saw that, once again, tears were streaming down his face. 'If you can't find your Mama and Dada, come back to me and I will mind you, I promise.'

Spotty was at the water's edge by now. He stopped for a second and looked back towards us. He honked once. 'He's saying goodbye,' said Michael. 'He's saying goodbye to me.'

Then Spotty gave a final scoot, and began to float. He flipped his tail and disappeared under the waves.

Poor Michael tried to be brave as I walked him back to the nursery, though I could see his little heart was broken.

* * *

A few days later, Lady Mary came back from visiting her sister, and that afternoon she sent for me. I felt nervous as I went to her study. Had she heard about my lies? Did she think I had forgotten all her kindness to me? Did she think I was an ungrateful girl, too ready to give up all the good things she had provided for me at Lissadell?

But Lady Mary smiled warmly at me, and even asked me to sit down.

'Mrs Bailey told me what happened while I was away,' she said. 'I can tell that your parents raised you to be a decent and honourable girl. If my children

grow up to be half the person you are, I shall be very proud indeed.'

'Thank you, Lady Mary,' I said.

'And there's something else I'd like to discuss with you,' she said.

'Yes, Lady Mary?'

'I have been speaking to Miss Connor in the needlework school, and she tells me that poor Miss Flanagan's mother remains very unwell.'

'I'm sorry to hear that.'

'Miss Connor and I have come to an arrangement with Miss Flanagan.'

I held my breath.

Why was she telling me this?

Was the arrangement something to do with me?

'As you know, the needlework school is closed on Saturdays and Sundays, and Miss Flanagan has asked if she could have Fridays off also, so she can help with the care of her mother. This presented a difficulty for Miss Connor, as there are so many women to train,

and so many orders to fill.'

Now I began to hope properly.

'So we would like if, for the coming months, you could spend Fridays helping Miss Connor at the needlework school. What would you think about that?'

I wanted to jump up on the table and dance a jig, but I held myself back.

'Thank you, Lady Mary,' I said politely. 'I would like that very much.'

But as soon as the words were out of my mouth I began to think of obstacles.

'But what about my work in the house? Will Nellie have to do everything, because that wouldn't be fair?'

'I have talked to Mrs Bailey. Delia can work with Nellie on Fridays.'

'But am I good enough? I can do hemming, and simple stitches like that, but what if the women need me to teach them complicated lace-work or smocking? I'm not sure I ...'

Lady Mary smiled at me. 'Please don't worry about

that,' she said. 'Miss Connor tells me you are very able, and I trust her judgement. She is confident that if she shows you something once, you will easily manage to share your new skill with the women.'

'Thank you, Lady Mary.'

'Oh – there's one last thing. On Fridays you won't be an under-housemaid any more – you will be an assistant needlework instructor.'

'Assistant needlework instructor!' I repeated the words after her, enjoying the feel of them in my mouth, loving the way they made me sound so important.

'Needlework instructors are paid more than house-maids,' she said. 'So you will see an increase in your wages from this Friday. Now, are we in agreement?'

'Yes, Lady Mary. I agree with all my heart.'

* * *

When Friday came around I put on my clean dress,

and brushed my hair a hundred times. I walked out of the house, and across to the coach-house court-yard. I felt nervous and excited as I went through the door and up the stairs.

Once again, the warmth and cheer of the room wrapped itself around me. Some of the women were singing, and some were talking quietly.

Miss Connor nodded to me. 'It's nice to have you back, Lily,' she said. 'You know what to do?'

'Yes,' I said, as I went to the corner where my group of women was sitting.

'Oh, 'tis yourself, Lily,' said Mary-Kate when she saw me. 'It does my heart good to see you. I wouldn't say a word against dear Miss Flanagan, but you, sure you're the best teacher in all the land.'

I smiled, as I took my seat next to her. 'Let me see what you're working on,' I said. She held it out to me, and I could see that while it was far from perfect, she had done her very best.

'Look at you,' I said. 'So good, so soon! Miss

Connor had better watch out, or you'll be after her job.'

She put her head down shyly, but I could see she was pleased.

The day flew by, and I could hardly believe how lucky I was to be paid good money for doing a job I loved so much.

My dream was still to teach little children to read and write, but this was one very small step in the right direction.

* * *

Maeve appeared unexpectedly the next day, and after dinner she came to my room. I was so happy to see my dear friend, I almost forgot it was so strange for a rich girl like her to be in a servant's bedroom.

'This is nice and cosy,' she said.

She was right. It wasn't big and fancy like her bedroom, but it was a warm and happy place. Maeve sat

beside me on my bed, and I wrapped Mam's shawl around our shoulders. Johanna and Nellie were already in their nightgowns, cuddled up together in Nellie's bed.

Nellie put aside the story she had been reading and picked up her songbook.

'Will we sing this one?' she said. '"When Irish Eyes are Smiling"? I hear it's a big hit all over the world.'

'And most of all here in Lissadell,' said Johanna with a smile.

And the four of us sang and laughed and talked until it was time for Johanna and Maeve to go to their own rooms. Then I put out the gaslight, and Nellie and I held hands for a moment as we settled down for another night in Lissadell.

Workhouses in Ireland

The first workhouses in Ireland opened in the 1840s, to deal with the many poor and starving people in the country. Eventually there were 163, each holding up to a thousand people.

Conditions were very harsh – families were separated into areas for men, women, boys and girls, though babies could stay with their mothers. Some workhouses allowed families to spend a little time together once a week, but some children never again saw their parents after arriving at the workhouse.

Everyone wore a uniform and slept on rough straw mattresses laid in rows on timber platforms.

They ate 'stirabout' (a kind of porridge), buttermilk, bread and potatoes. Most people got a little meat or a piece of sweet cake as a treat at Christmas and Easter. Meals were eaten in silence.

Adults and children were expected to work hard. Sometimes this meant breaking stones, and building roads that went nowhere.

Even children were punished harshly for breaking the rules. One punishment book has the following record:

Name	Offence	Punishment
William McElhinney	Gave a boy a kick	Whipped
John Goodwin	Exhibiting bad temper	No Supper
Patrick Maguire	Sleeping in church	No supper

People could leave at any time, but most had nowhere to go.

The last workhouses in Ireland closed in the 1920s. Many of the buildings were later used as hospitals or homes for old people.

Portumna Workhouse, Co. Galway. Photograph by Carsten Krieger.

The Gore-Booth Family

Josslyn and Mary Gore-Booth had eight children, four of whom had been born at the time this story takes place. These were Maeve de Markievicz's first cousins.

Michael, Brian, Hugh, Brigid, Rosaleen, Aideen, Gabrielle and Angus Gore-Booth. Photograph from the Lissadell Collection

Michael (1908-1987)

In this book we meet Michael as a little boy. As an adult, he had some mental health difficulties, and so didn't inherit the title and estate at Lissadell (as it was decided he would be unable to manage). He spent his adult life in hospital in York in England; his parents and siblings visited him regularly. The Gore-Booth children really did have a pet seal who they kept in the pond, though in reality it was at a slightly later date than in this story.

Hugh (1910-1943)

Hugh loved fishing and studying birds, and went to Oxford University to study rural economy and agriculture. He loved to travel, visiting Sweden and Lapland on fishing holidays. In 1939, at the start of World War Two, he joined the Irish Fusiliers. He died in action on the island of Leros. His father, Josslyn, died four days after he received the news. It was said at the time that he died of a broken heart.

Bridget (1911-1992)

Like her Aunt Constance, Bridget grew up to be a noted artist, and much of her work was inspired by the landscape around Lissadell. During World War Two, she spent time in rural England, taking care of children who had been evacuated from London to escape German bombing raids.

Brian (1912-1940)

As a young man, Brian joined the Royal Navy – maybe not a good idea, as he often suffered from sea-sickness! In 1936 he left and set up a business as a literary agent. In 1939, a month after the start of the war, he was called up to rejoin the navy. In 1940, his ship was torpedoed and Brian was killed along with all of the crew. Before news of this reached his mother, she wrote to him telling him that she had sent a parcel containing

a cake. Later the letter was returned to Lissadell, stamped –
Return to Sender – admiralty instruction.

Rosaleen (1914-1991)

Like many of the Gore-Booths, she loved painting and horses,
and was an expert needleworker. When she died she was
buried in the family plot at Lissadell, as were her three sisters.

Aideen (1916-1994)

Aideen was a keen swimmer, often swimming twice a day, even
into old age. She was tutored at home, and was then sent to
a 'finishing school' in London with her sister Gabrielle. She
worked for a time as a children's nurse in England and Ireland. Once at a dinner party she was asked, 'What relation
was that harridan Countess Markievicz to you?' She replied,
'She was my aunt, and she had the courage of her convictions.'
Aideen spent her later years in Lissadell with Gabrielle; by
then the house was crumbling around them, the garden was
overgrown, and the main avenue was full of potholes. Aideen
and Gabrielle lived in the bedrooms and a small kitchen, with
the rest of the house abandoned. By then it was damp and cold,
but Aideen gave guided tours to save money to keep the roof
watertight.

Gabrielle (1918-1973)

Gabrielle was very close to her sister Aideen. They often went on cycling tours around Ireland. Gabrielle loved music and played the organ in Lissadell Church. When her father died, Gabrielle took over the running of Lissadell Estate. There were many legal issues and the once-prosperous estate fell into disarray.

Angus (1920-1996)

Angus served in the Irish Guards during World War Two. Unlike his two older brothers, he made it home, but was traumatised by his experiences. He lived his later years with his sisters Gabrielle and Aideen in Lissadell. Angus was the only one of the eight siblings to have children, and when he died, the house and the title passed to his son, Josslyn Henry. In 2003, Josslyn Henry sold the estate to the current owners, Constance Cassidy and Edward Walsh. Until then, the house had been owned by the Gore-Booth family for 406 years!

These are some of the books and websites that helped in my research for this book:

Irishworkhousecentre.ie

Irishamerica.com

Discoverireland.ie

Workhouses of the North West edited by Jack Johnston

Grim Bastilles of Despair by Paschal Mahoney

The Gore-Booths of Lissadell by Dermot James

Maeve de Markievicz by Clive Scoular

Blazing a Trail by Sarah Webb and Lauren O'Neill

Acknowledgements

I'd like to thank Dan, Brian, Ellen and Annie for their ongoing love and support.

Thanks to all the lovely booksellers, librarians and teachers who have been so positive and kind about Lily, and my first step into historical fiction.

Thanks to the wonderful team at O'Brien Press for another great production; special thanks to my editor, Helen.

Thanks to Rachel Corcoran for a beautiful cover.

Thanks to Lissadell House for all the help with history, geography and photographs. If there are mistakes in this book, it's definitely not your fault!